"Yes, it was a proposal," Jessica snapped back

She was furious at Sam's laughter. "I'd do anything to save McGill Construction— even marry you!"

"Put like that, how can I refuse?" Sam drawled with a mocking smile.

"Well, you needn't keep laughing about it," she snarled. "You can just forget I ever said it."

"But I've accepted," Sam replied smoothly. "You offered me something I might have had to wait twenty years for—to head my own construction company."

A wave of weakness nearly knocked Jessica off her feet. "You what?" she gasped. "You really are cold-blooded."

"Then that makes two of us, doesn't it?" Sam countered. "We should be well matched, my dear."

What had she done? She must have been mad! And Sam Ryder, too, for that matter.

D0834357

her back, and his hands were almost suffocating

SUSANNE McCARTHY has spent most of her life in London, but after her marriage she and her husband moved to Shropshire, and the author is now an enthusiastic advocate of this unspoiled part of England. So although her first romance novel, *A Long Way from Heaven*, was set in the sunny Caribbean, Susanne says that the English countryside may feature in her future writing.

Books by Susanne McCarthy

HARLEQUIN PRESENTS

Don't miss any of our special offers. Write to us at the following address for information on our newest releases.

Harlequin Reader Service
901 Fuhrmann Blvd., P.O. Box 1397, Buffalo, NY 14240
Canadian address: P.O. Box 603,
Fort Erie, Ont. L2A 5X3

SUSANNE McCARTHY

too much to lose

Harlequin Books

TORONTO • NEW YORK • LONDON
AMSTERDAM • PARIS • SYDNEY • HAMBURG
STOCKHOLM • ATHENS • TOKYO • MILAN

Harlequin Presents first edition November 1988
ISBN 0-373-11123-1

Original hardcover edition published in 1987
by Mills & Boon Limited

CHAPTER ONE

'How do you think the men'll take to the idea of working for a woman then, Sam?'

Sam Ryder shrugged his wide shoulders non-committally as he moved with a sure-footed step from the scaffolding into the cage, and pulled the lever to lower it to the ground. 'She won't try to keep it on,' he concluded. 'She'll sell out to one of the big conglomerates.'

The cage landed with a gentle thump on the well trodden ground at the base of the half-finished building, and the two men walked over to the hut nearby. As Sam pushed the door open he laughed drily. 'Anyway,' he added, 'can you imagine a woman like that picking her way around a building-site?'

On the wall opposite the door was a pin-up, torn from a magazine. The girl was beautiful. Her mouth curved with delicate sensuality, and her eyes were the colour of the sea. She was kneeling on a satin-covered bed, her wild auburn curls tossed around her slim shoulders. She was wearing a skimpy thing of silk and lace, but the effect was more devastating than if she had been naked.

'Who put that thing up there anyway, Fred?'

The site manager laughed. 'It was someone's idea of a joke. It's been on the back of the door in the tea-shed for ages. Angus never saw it.'

'Just as well. He'd have blown a gasket.'

Fred chuckled. '"Jezebel",' he read from the caption under the pin-up. 'She looks a real hell-cat, don't she? It'd take a rare man to tame that one.'

Sam's head was bent over the drawings on the table. 'If her father and two husbands couldn't do it, any man who tries has to be crazy,' he remarked dismissively. 'We're falling behind on this section, Fred. What's the problem?'

'Suppliers. We were promised the RSJs two weeks ago, but first they said the lorry had broken down, then they'd got a problem with the computer.'

'Well, tell them if they're not here tomorrow we'll buy elsewhere. I'm not being pushed into penalty time for something I can practically pick up in the High Street.'

'*You're* not?' teased Fred gently.

Sam grinned wryly. 'All right, McGill Construction isn't. Old habits die hard.'

'Not been a very good year for you, has it, Sam?' remarked Fred sympathetically, setting down a big white china mug in front of him.

Sam stuck his pencil behind his ear and picked up his tea. 'I'm not complaining,' he said levelly. 'I'm not the only builder who's gone bust—not by a long chalk.'

'But then you came to work for Angus, and now that he's dead . . .'

Sam laughed rather harshly. 'Oh, he was bound to get himself killed like that, sooner or later. Angus's idea about roads was—he built it, he owned it. And no forty-ton truck was going to tell him different.'

Fred nodded thoughtfully. 'I suppose you're right. It seems a funny thing that a guy like Angus should only have a daughter to follow him. Somehow you'd think he'd be the type to produce half a dozen strapping great sons.'

'From what I hear of her,' commented Sam, glancing speculatively at the pin-up again, 'one daughter was more than enough—even for Angus!'

The sleek red Porsche Targa wove skilfully through the heavy rush-hour traffic. Jess had left the roof down, defying the unpredictable weather of an English summertime. She just wanted to feel the wind in her hair. Her spirit was restless, unable to find peace. She had been shattered by her father's sudden death— Angus had seemed immortal, invincible. And though they had fought like cat and dog, she had adored him.

And yet, in a strange kind of way, it was as if she had been set free. All her life, every action had been dictated by him—either struggling to please him, or racing off in defiance to do something stupid. Now she would... Damn! The traffic lights ahead had changed to red. She braked smoothly, and pulled up next to a muddy Land Rover.

She was playing one of her favourite rock-music tapes loudly on the car stereo, and tapping her fingers lightly on the steering-wheel in time to the pounding beat. Slowly she became aware that she was being subjected to an appreciative survey from the driver of the Land Rover.

She was accustomed to being stared at in that way, and she tilted her chin at a proud angle, looking straight ahead and trying to ignore him. But somehow her eyes were drawn towards him. He was certainly good-looking, though there was a hint of arrogance in the hard line of his jaw. His dark hair was slightly ruffled, and his skin had the sort of tan that came from spending most of his time out of doors. His eyes were grey, and there was a mocking smile in them that made hers flash with cold disdain.

He saluted her sardonically, and as the lights changed put his car in gear—and cut straight across into her lane! She peeped her horn furiously, but she couldn't get past him. He turned into the same multistorey car park that she was going to use, and she followed him up the ramp, seething with suppressed rage.

The car park was already quite full, and they had to climb through several floors before there was even one space. The Land Rover pulled forward to reverse into it, and with a smile of grim satisfaction Jess put her foot down hard on the accelerator, and slipped her car neatly into the space.

He blasted his horn loudly, but she merely smiled sweetly at him as she leaned over to pick up her briefcase. The Land Rover shot away and up the next ramp. Jess guessed that he was going to come back and yell at her, but she had no intention of running away. Taking her time, she checked her make-up, straightened the emerald green silk scarf at her throat, and brushed down her smart French navy business suit before walking calmly towards the steps.

She had almost reached the bottom when she heard him above her, coming down two steps at a time. Schooling her features into an expression of calm composure, she carried on walking. In a few seconds he caught up with her, and blocked her way with his arm. She paused, and swept him a haughty gaze from those sea-green eyes. He was a big man; she was tall, and he was standing on the step below her, yet she still had to look up at him. But she refused to be intimidated.

'You took my parking space,' he accused. His grey eyes gleamed with mocking amusement, and she wondered what he found so funny.

She shrugged her slim shoulders in cool indifference. 'First come, first served,' she retorted.

'But *I* was there first.'

'So you were.'

'What are you going to do about it?' he enquired.

She lifted one finely drawn eyebrow in faint contempt. 'What am *I* going to do? I don't see why I should do anything.'

'But I'm very angry.' He swung round, leaning his other hand on the wall to cage her between his two arms. But it wasn't anger in the grey eyes that looked down into hers.

'I'm terrified,' she murmured mockingly, meeting his gaze without wavering.

'So you should be.'

His eyes had focused speculatively on her lips, and for a brief moment she was tempted to wait and see if he was going to try to kiss her. But she really had no wish to be mauled about by some big ape in a car park, so she ducked smoothly under his arm and walked on down the steps. 'Then I suggest you go and take it out on a punch-bag,' she tossed back at him. 'There's a boxing-gym round the corner.' As she stepped out into the street she heard his rich laughter echoing in the stairwell.

* * *

The office that had been her father's was on the fourth floor of a small office block he had built himself, just round the corner from the Elephant and Castle. Jess loved to watch the traffic streaming round the vast roundabouts, coming in from Southwark and Lambeth and peeling off to head for Westminster or the City. At night the lights reflected romantically in the bright steel prisms in the centre of the islands; by day it was the hot red of the London buses, the blues and greens and yellows of the cars.

Reluctantly she turned from the window, and sat down at the big leather-topped desk. There was so much to come to grips with! Contracts, tenders and suppliers, and technical jargon that she didn't really understand, although she had listened intently to her father's talk ever since she came up to his knee.

But though she was no civil engineer, she *did* know how to run a business—which seemed to be more than could be said for Angus. Dear Angus—he had been a builder, most at home laying a new motorway or watching an office-block rise thirty storeys to the sky. He had never enjoyed the paper-work side as the firm had got bigger and bigger.

Not that her little graphic design agency bore much resemblance to McGill Construction. But at least it had been doing well—or it would have been if that unfortunate copyright suit hadn't virtually wiped her out. But that was yesterday's news now. She wouldn't have time to run the agency in tandem with McGill Construction, so she would have to wind it up.

She had no illusions about the task she had taken on. If only she had been born a boy! Angus had never let her become involved with the firm—he had always insisted that the construction industry was no place for a woman. Well, she would show him ...

A sad little smile curved her mouth. How often had she said that? Though Angus was gone, old habits lingered. Perhaps if she had had a mother, things might have been different. But her mother had died when she was a baby, and there had been no one to come between father and daughter when they were having one of their frequent spats. And all her life she seemed to have been lurching from one disaster to the next.

There had been her first marriage—how she blushed at the memory of that now! She had been so naïve— just eighteen, and still at school. Maybe if Angus hadn't taken such a strong dislike to Gary, she would not have fancied herself so much in love with him, would not have been so blind. 'You're such a snob— just because his father's the school gardener!' she had shouted at him. 'Well, Gary loves me, and I love him. And anyway, I'm eighteen now—I can do what I like.'

They had made their plans in secret, thinking themselves terribly clever. Gary had got a special licence, using his mother's address so that no one would find out. Straight after the wedding she had phoned Angus in triumph from a call-box across the road from the register office, and he had retaliated by immediately stating his intention of cutting off her allowance and cutting her out of his will.

He had meant it, too, but she had just laughed at him. But Gary hadn't thought it was very funny. He had stalked off to the pub in a huff, accusing Jess of provoking Angus. He had carried on drinking for the rest of the day, and the wedding night she had looked forward to with such shy excitement had been spent crying on her own in the hotel room. At one o'clock in the morning she had got a taxi home. Angus had let her in, grim-faced, and the marriage had quietly been annulled.

That experience had made her wary of men, and she had decided to launch herself instead on a modelling career. She had started off quite well—her rich auburn hair had been much in demand for shampoo ads, and she was fortunate that her fair skin was creamy rather than freckled. There had even been talk of a television commercial. Until she had taken that lingerie job.

She had barely given it a second thought at the time. She hadn't done lingerie work before, but she had done quite a lot of swimwear work. She had worked with the photographer several times, and 'Jezebel' was a very stylish range of lingerie. It had been a good session, the photographer had been pleased with her work—it had seemed like a straightforward job, just like any other.

She had been stunned when she had seen the prints. She had never dreamed that they would come out so... erotic. Of course she should have known—she was an experienced model, she knew the effects of lighting, she knew the way her face looked through the eye of the camera. No one had believed her when she had protested her innocence.

She had tried to brave it out. But though she was offered plenty of work, it wasn't the sort of work she had wanted to do. The agency hadn't been very pleased with her when she had steadfastly turned the offers down. But worse was the way everybody, even the paper-boy and the greengrocer, began treating her... differently. Though she had never posed nude—not even topless—it was as if she had featured as the centrefold of one of those magazines they keep on the top shelf in the newsagents.

There was only one man who hadn't treated her as if she were fair game—Douglas, her second husband. He had been a rather mediocre painter when she had met him, but he had a real flair for colour, and she had coaxed him into doing some design work for another friend, who had a small business.

One thing had led to another. Soon she had found herself setting up an agency, helping Douglas and his friends earn pin-money by using her contacts in the world of commerce. And somehow she had managed to delude herself that the gentle friendship she shared with Douglas would be a good foundation for marriage.

It hadn't, of course. Poor Douglas—she should have left him with his dreams. He had been quite overpowered by the reality. Maybe if she had been as experienced as everyone assumed, it might have turned out better, but the fact was it had been a miserable disaster, right from their wedding night, when the experienced woman he had expected had turned out to be nothing of the kind.

It had suited them both to keep up the pretence for a while, but eventually he had met a sweet-natured, motherly girl who had been just what he needed. So they had had an amicable divorce—she hadn't wanted to embarrass him with an annulment, and everyone assumed her first marriage had ended in divorce anyway, so it didn't make much difference.

So here she was, twenty-six years old, and from now on she was on her own, with only herself to blame if she made a hash of it. She *would* succeed—if only to prove to herself that she could do one thing right.

With a small sigh she set her memories aside. She had a great deal to do—there was all this paperwork, and she had an important meeting in a little while. She pressed the button of the intercom on her desk with one plum-red fingertip. 'Fiona, has Bill sent in those cost estimates yet?' she asked.

'No, I'm sorry, Jessica, he hasn't,' her secretary responded. 'Would you like me to go and fetch them?'

'That shouldn't be necessary. Can't his secretary bring them to you?'

'Bill always stalls until you hold your hand out,' Fiona advised her with a chuckle. 'He thinks that makes everybody believe he's snowed under with work.'

Jess laughed. 'OK, Fiona, if you've got time. Go and give his poor ego a rub.' Fiona was a blessing. She had been Angus's secretary for twenty years, and what she didn't know about the firm, and the personalities and foibles of the people who worked for it and dealt with it, wasn't worth knowing. Jess had wondered how Fiona would take to the unexpected advent of a young woman at the helm, but unlike some of the male staff, Fiona had done everything she could to help the new boss.

Jess continued sorting through the day's mail. Some of it could be fairly quickly dealt with by a short answering letter, and she picked up her Dictaphone and leaned back in the deep leather executive chair. But there wasn't a tape in the machine, and she didn't have one in her drawer either. Cursing her own inefficiency, she went out into Fiona's office to see if she could find one.

There were none on top of the desk, so she stretched across and opened the top drawer to see if that was where Fiona kept them. She was rummaging among the pencils and Tipp-Ex when she felt the sharp imprint of a hand across her round *derrière*. She straightened and turned in indignant fury, to find herself confronting the man who had been driving the Land Rover.

'I'm sorry,' he said, his taunting smile robbing his words of any trace of apology. 'I couldn't resist it.'

'How dare you?' she gasped. In spite of the lightness of his manner, he somehow exuded a powerful aura of masculinity which forced her into retreat.

'Well, you did steal my parking space,' he reminded her, that maddening gleam of amusement lighting his grey eyes. 'I warned you that I was very angry.'

'I've a good mind to . . .'

'Yes?'

'Call the police!'

'They might want to view the evidence.'

Her cheeks flamed scarlet, and she retreated a pace further. 'Get out of my office, you big ape,' she insisted tensely.

'But I've only just arrived.'

'I've got nothing to say to you. Go away.'

He sat back against the desk, his arms folded across his wide chest, so infuriatingly sure of himself that her palm itched to slap him. 'Heaven preserve me from contrary females,' he drawled. 'You invited me up here...'

'I invited you up here?' she protested hotly. 'You followed me!'

'My, you do think you're the bee's knees, don't you?' he taunted.

She took a deep, steadying breath, fighting to suppress the blazing fury that was threatening to explode inside her skull. 'Look, Mr... whatever your name is—I have to admit that you don't look insane, so maybe it's me that's round the bend, but I'm afraid I have no recollection whatsoever of inviting you up here.'

'Oh, you didn't invite me personally,' he informed her calmly. 'Your secretary rang me yesterday, and so of course I came hot-foot to obey your command.' He held out his hand to her, a disarming grin on his handsome face. 'My name's Sam Ryder.'

Jess froze in anger. He worked for her; Angus had taken him on just three months ago, to be a kind of trouble-shooter, realising—a little belatedly—that he was not the best person to deal with situations that needed cool handling. He was vital to her plans. But if he thought she was just going to forget his insolent behaviour... She drew herself up haughtily, ignoring his proffered hand. 'I see,' she responded in arctic tones. 'Well, would you kindly take a seat, Mr Ryder? I will see you in a few minutes.'

She turned her back on him, and marched back into her own office, closing the door firmly behind her. She realised suddenly that she was trembling from head to foot. Damn the man! She had meant to be so charming to him, to get him on her side... and instead he had made her lose her temper.

She walked over to the window and stared down blankly into the street. Well, she had got off to a very bad start, but somehow she would have to try to regain her dignity. Should she demand an apology from him? After all, he had treated her abominably... at least, he had patted her on the bottom. Maybe it wasn't really so awful, looked at objectively—it was probably his clumsy way of trying to flirt with her. If she stayed angry, wouldn't she just look like a humourless bitch?

Oh, dammit—she was just going round in circles. Shaking her head impatiently, she moved hesitantly back to the door and pulled it open. He was lounging back at his ease in Fiona's chair, his feet on her desk. Jess repressed a fresh surge of annoyance. 'I'm sorry to have kept you waiting, Mr Ryder,' she said, as formally polite as if they had never met before. 'Would you come in now, please?'

His steely eyes subjected her to a lazy scrutiny, but though his mouth still wore that mocking smile, she sensed a dangerous anger lurking just beneath the surface. 'Two things, Miss McGill,' he said. 'One, I'm the Chief Engineer. I don't appreciate being kept cooling my heels as if I were the window-cleaner.'

'If you will try to behave like a chief engineer instead of a window-cleaner, I will try to remember,' she retaliated crisply.

He inclined his head in acknowledgement. 'Two— why hasn't the tender gone off to TDC yet?'

'I'm waiting for the costings from Bill French.'

He made an impatient noise in his throat. 'If you're going to sit at that desk filing your nails all day, you might as well call in the liquidators on the company right away,' he said. 'It's your job to see that bids get out on time. If you miss the deadline on a big tender like that, it's no good weeping or fluttering your eye-lashes—the job's lost.'

'I have no intention of conducting myself in that way,' she rapped, leashing her temper with difficulty. 'Fiona has gone to fetch the schedule now, and I would like to go through the whole thing with you before it goes out in today's post.'

'Good.' He unfolded himself from the chair. 'Let's get down to business then, shall we?'

They spent the whole morning discussing every contract that McGill was currently working on or tendering for. Jess couldn't help but be impressed by Sam's knowledge. He had every detail at his fingertips. She couldn't complain of his manners now, either—he was punctilious about acknowledging that she was the boss, and treated her with just the right amount of respect.

'Well, that's about it,' she said at last. 'Thank you very much, Sam. I think that's a good morning's work.'

He flexed his arms, stretching the muscles across his wide back. 'How about some lunch?' he suggested.

Jess felt suddenly nervous. Having, she felt, established her position here in the office, she was reluctant to risk it by stepping outside with him. 'Where were you thinking of going?' she asked a little defensively.

'There's a pub round the corner that does a decent bar-snack—if that's not too rough-and-ready for you?'

'Of course not,' she countered quickly. 'It certainly isn't worth going all the way into town just to have lunch.'

'Right.' He stood up, and grinned down at her. 'Come on, then.'

Jess hesitated. His physical presence seemed to dominate the office. But it was her office! He was the one who knew their suppliers by their first names, knew who else would be tendering for the same contracts and what their prices would be. He had chosen where they were going for lunch. He was in control, and she resented it.

'I don't know,' she demurred. 'I don't think I've really got time for lunch. Perhaps I'll just ask Fiona to bring me in some sandwiches.'

'Rubbish. You've got to eat. You're doing a proper job now, not just pouting for the cameras.' He took her arm, and lifted her to her feet. She glared up at him angrily. 'Don't argue with me,' he advised, an inflection of amusement in his voice. 'It's only lunch.'

Weakly, she conceded. 'Very well. Now will you please let go of my arm?'

He released her, but as she moved past him, he gave her another intimate little pat on the behind. She jerked round quickly, her eyes blazing. He held up his hands in a poor imitation of innocence. 'Sorry!'

She tilted her chin at a proud angle, and turning on her heel stalked from the room.

The pub was fairly crowded, but they managed to find a table to sit at. Jess had often lunched there with her father, and it brought back a lot of memories. She was going to miss him dreadfully. She toyed with her salad, not having much appetite.

'What's wrong?'

'What? Oh ... I was just thinking about Angus,' she said. 'It seems sort of funny to be coming in here without him.'

'It must have come as quite a shock to you,' he remarked.

She glanced up at him cautiously, but she could detect no trace of mockery in his eyes. 'Yes, it was,' she agreed, the sadness in her heart echoing in her voice. 'It's going to take a lot of getting used to.'

'Were you fond of him?'

Her eyes flashed indignantly. 'Of course I was. What a thing to say! He was my father.'

'I shouldn't think he was a very easy person to have for a father,' he mused.

'I really wouldn't know,' she responded in arctic tones. 'He was the only one I had, so I've nothing to compare him with.'

Sam laughed gently. 'Don't get upset. I only meant that he had a very strong personality. I had a great deal of respect for him.'

Jess gave him a steady look from those sea-green eyes. 'Most people thought he was a tyrant.'

Sam shook his head. 'Not a tyrant, no. I'm not saying he was the most diplomatic person I've ever met. But he was in a tough business. He'd never have built a firm like McGill if he'd been chicken-hearted.'

Jess saw a chance to even up the score a little. 'You weren't so lucky, were you?' she enquired, her mouth curving into a taunting smile.

But Sam Ryder wasn't an easy man to ruffle. He shrugged his wide shoulders in casual dismissal. 'I wasn't,' he agreed cordially. 'I took one risk too many.'

'What happened?' she asked, drawn by curiosity.

'I took on too many big contracts in Central America, and got my fingers burned—almost literally. They decided to start a war.'

'You lost a lot of money?'

'You can't pack up a twenty-storey building and carry it home.'

'No, I suppose not. Couldn't you get any compensation?'

'I'm working on it,' he told her grimly. 'Meantime I had to wind up all my other operations—it was that or go bankrupt. Angus took over a couple of my contracts.'

'Didn't you resent that?'

Again he shrugged. 'Why should I? It wasn't his fault. And if he could drive a hard bargain, at least he was an honest man. That's why I agreed to come and work for him.'

Jess sipped her dry martini thoughtfully. 'You don't think I can hack it, do you?' she asked.

'I didn't say so.'

'You didn't have to—I can read between the lines.'

He smiled at her, as if to take the sting out of his words. 'OK, since you ask—no, I don't think you can hack it. And not just because you don't know how to put one brick on top of another—you employ people like me to deal with that side of things.'

'So what's going to stop me doing as good a job as my father?'

'Look, most of the consultant engineers responsible for letting the big contracts are going to be very wary of you. They probably won't even invite you to tender—at least until they see which way the wind's blowing.'

'Oh, I get it,' she commented tartly. 'It's all the old-pals act, isn't it? And they won't let a woman into their club.'

He shrugged. 'As I said—it's a tough business. And then there's the labour-force—maybe it's an old fashioned attitude, but a lot of the men won't like working for a woman.'

Jess felt a bitter anger seething inside her. He sounded just like Angus! 'You think I'm going to let a stupid bunch of male chauvinists get the better of me?' she demanded. 'You'll see.'

'If you're wise you'll sell out now,' he advised her seriously. 'You stand to lose a lot of money if the firm folds.'

She shook her head. 'The money isn't important,' she told him firmly. 'I can't just give up. The McGill name is going to stay in the construction business, or I'm not a McGill!'

He laughed. 'Oh, you're a McGill all right—red-haired and pig-headed. And you're going to fall flat on your beautiful face.'

Her eyes glittered with determination as she looked across the table at him. 'Don't bet on that,' she advised him grimly.

A slow smile curved his hard mouth. 'Well, it should be interesting to watch, anyway,' he drawled laconically.

CHAPTER TWO

'I DON'T really think I'm in the mood for Lisa's party tonight.'

Mark—her current escort—stared at her in astonishment. 'Not in the mood? Come off it, Jess! It'll be a great party. Everyone'll be there.'

Jess yawned. 'I've been working all week,' she protested.

'All work and no play... Come on, let's just go for a little while. We can always leave early if it's a bore.'

'Oh, all right, if you're so keen,' she conceded. 'You'll have to wait while I go and put something more partyish on, though. Help yourself to a drink.'

Jess had kept her London flat. The big house in Surrey, where Angus had lived, seemed so sad and empty without him. She hadn't quite made up her mind what to do about it yet—the sensible thing would be to sell it, but that seemed a little too... final. So she had postponed making any decision for the time being.

She liked her flat. It was on the top floor of a tall, modern block, and afforded her spectacular views over the grey-brown patchwork of south London, with the River Thames threading through like a steel ribbon. She had had the lounge decorated in dazzling white, hung with a selection of paintings she had bought from the artists who displayed their work along Green Park railings every Sunday morning.

Her bedroom, by contrast, was done in a soft, restful pale green, and the furniture was good reproduction Sheraton, with one or two genuine pieces. Her wardrobe exhibited a similar dichotomy—some of her dresses were elegant and sophisticated, some were stunning and outrageous.

She cast her eyes along the row of dresses, trying to decide what to wear. Maybe if she wore something jazzy it would put her in the party mood. And anyway, since it was Lisa's party, she might as well live up to her 'bad girl' reputation. Lisa wouldn't let her do anything else.

Lisa's father had been one of Angus's best friends and greatest rivals, and the two girls had been at school together. Lisa was a year younger than Jess; a sweet, dainty little blonde with sapphire-blue eyes and a mouth that butter wouldn't melt in. And a line in sneakiness that would make a serpent blush.

Somehow, ever since she was twelve, whenever there had been trouble Lisa had always been right in the thick of it, and had always come up smelling of roses—while Jess had usually found herself knee-deep in the other thing! It was Lisa, she was certain, who had made sure Angus found out all about Gary—and Lisa who had spun luridly embroidered tales of the run-away marriage among all their friends.

And Lisa always had a way of making sure that those lingerie adverts were never quite forgotten—she had coined the nickname 'Jezebel' from them, and the image had stuck. But Jess daren't let Lisa guess how she really felt about those awful pictures—then she would really have got some enjoyment from her endless needling. So, unable to live it down, she was forced to brazen it out.

With cool deliberation she chose a shimmering sheath of blue-green sequins, cut dashingly off one shoulder and moulding every contour of her body. It called for strong make-up, and she sat down at her dressing table to achieve a work of art, calling on all the skill of her modelling training. She swept her hair up into a thick hank on one side of her head, arranging it in a fall of curls over one ear. She would wear no jewellery—that would have made her look like a Christmas tree—but she wound a long feather boa, perfectly dyed to match the dress, around her neck, and slipped her feet into a pair of high-heeled evening sandals.

'Wow!'

Jess laughed at Mark's reaction. 'Are you ready to go?' she asked.

'I don't think I want to go to the party now,' he said. 'I'd much rather stay here and make love to you.'

'Not tonight,' she demurred with a sweet smile as she invited him to help her into her velvet jacket.

'You always say that,' he protested sulkily.

'Of course.'

He caught her arm. 'Just tell me one thing,' he demanded sharply. 'Are you sleeping with anyone else?'

She thought of telling him to mind his own business, but he looked so unhappy that she relented. 'No, Mark,' she promised softly, kissing him lightly on the cheek. 'Just be patient with me, please. I haven't had much luck with men so far, and I'm not really ready to commit myself again.'

He wrapped his arms around her, and drew her close. 'You could trust me, Jess,' he whispered urgently. 'You know I'm in love with you.'

She rested her head against his shoulder for a moment, but then drew back out of his arms. 'You're very sweet, Mark, and I'm very fond of you, but . . . oh, come on, let's go to the party, shall we?'

Lisa's flat was in the basement of her parents' Belgravia house. The pulsing sound of loud rock-music could be heard as soon as the taxi turned the corner, and as Mark had said, everyone was there. Lisa was looking girlishly demure in a floating white dress, her hair artlessly curling around her shoulders.

'Jez! Oh, I'm so glad you came. You look *sensational*—I wish I had the nerve to wear a dress like that.'

Jess gritted her teeth into a brittle smile. Of all Lisa's annoying little tricks, her worst was that subtle elision, changing her name from Jessica to Jezebel. It put her constantly on the defensive. 'I wouldn't have missed it for the world!' she murmured insincerely as Lisa kissed her cheek. 'Marianne told me you've got a new boyfriend.'

'Oh, yes! But of course, you know him already— he works for you.'

Jess froze, sensing that sardonic gaze resting on her even before she looked up to see him lounging in the doorway. He was looking casually relaxed in a dark blue check shirt, open at the collar, and rough denim jeans; but something about him seemed to make all the other men in their trendy tee-shirts or smart evening clothes appear thin and pasty by comparison.

Lisa drew him forward, and nestled up to him, sweeping him an adoring gaze from those limpid blue eyes. He dropped an arm around her shoulders, and gave her an affectionate squeeze. Jess surveyed the pair of them coldly. She was a little surprised that a seemingly intelligent man like Sam should fall for a sugary doll like Lisa, but if that was his taste...

'Good evening, Sam,' she greeted him with formal politeness. 'I don't believe you've met Mark Hollis, have you?'

Sam extended his hand with a friendly grin. 'Pleased to meet you,' he said genially.

Mark shook his hand, muttering something appropriate, but Jess sensed a stiffness in him. She hoped he wasn't going to enter into some sort of stupid male rivalry with Sam. After all, it was quite unnecessary—he was just as attractive, just as manly...only in a different sort of way.

Jess took his arm. 'Come and get me a drink, Mark,' she urged. 'See you later, Lisa.'

To her relief, Mark didn't argue. They squeezed their way through the crush, leaving their coats with all the others in the spare bedroom, and went on to the kitchen where the sickly-sweet aroma of wine and beer hung heavily on the air.

'What do you want to drink?' asked Mark.

'I'll just have a white wine spritz, thank you.'

'I wonder if Lisa's got any Scotch in.' He went off to search among the bottles on the draining-board.

'Jess! You look terrific! How's the building-trade?'

Jess turned with a smile as one of her other friends hailed her. 'Hello, Ria. Oh, it's very hard work, but I'm enjoying it,' she answered.

'Does that hunk on Lisa's arm really work for you?'

Jess smiled wryly. 'Yes, he does—at the moment. I suspect Lisa may be trying to recruit him—in more ways than one.'

Ria glanced in the direction of that dark head, a little higher than those around him. 'Well, if I were you, I wouldn't let him go. He's *gorgeous*!' she declared. 'Is it true what Lisa's been telling me about him?'

'What's that?'

'The way he got his men out of Central America in the middle of a revolution? Lisa says they were trapped right in the middle of the fighting, and he flew a plane in himself and brought them out.' Ria sighed. 'He looks the type that would do a thing like that. Mmm—he could rescue me any day of the week!'

Jess laughed drily. 'I'm sure. All I want him to do is pour concrete for me.'

Ria giggled. 'Oh, you can play it cool,' she insisted, 'but I wouldn't mind betting you fancy him yourself.'

'He's not bad,' she conceded coolly. 'But I never mix business with pleasure. Ah, there you are, Mark,' she added as he returned with her drink. 'Shall we go and have a dance? It's a bit crowded here in the hall.'

It was crowded too in the big sitting-room, where couples were squashed up close to dance to the music pounding out of the stereo system. Conversation was difficult, but Mark put his mouth close to Jess's ear to ask, 'What does that chap do, then?'

'You mean Sam?' He nodded. 'He's my Chief Engineer. He goes round to all the sites, making sure everything is going smoothly.'

'So you work quite closely with him then?'

'Yes. Once I get into the swing of things I'll probably be meeting with him quite often,' she told him.

Mark's handsome face creased into a frown. 'You be careful of him,' he advised darkly. 'I didn't like the way he was looking at you.'

Jess repressed a surge of impatience. 'Oh, Mark, don't be silly. For one thing, he's going out with Lisa; and for another, I know how to handle men like Sam Ryder.'

'I wish you'd agree to at least get engaged to me,' he persisted. 'Then men like that would know to keep their hands off.'

She shook her head. 'No, Mark,' she insisted gently. 'I told you—I've been married twice, and I don't want to make a third mistake.'

'How do you know it would be a mistake?'

'Oh, please, Mark. Let's not discuss it now. You were the one who wanted to come to the party—let's just enjoy ourselves, eh?'

Unfortunately Mark's idea of enjoying himself was to hold her far closer than even the crush in the room made necessary, and to let his hands wander down her back in a way that annoyed her intensely. She was even more annoyed when she realised that Sam was watching from the doorway, his eyes in shadow, a mocking smile on his mouth.

Try as she might, she couldn't quite ignore him. She had to find a way of escape. She looked up at Mark with an appealing smile. 'Would you get me another drink, Mark?'

'What? OK—I could do with another one myself.'

Released from that encroaching embrace, she began to ease her way over to the far side of the room, but she was accosted by another friend. 'Jess! Looking like a million dollars, as usual. Come and have a dance with me.' So she moved back into the crush, and turning her back on those grey eyes watching her so steadily she let her body sway to the rhythm of the music.

She knew a lot of people at the party, and a lot of the men wanted to dance with her. She flirted with them, and laughed at their jokes, but all the time she was aware of Sam, and wondered with a touch of apprehension if he would come over and dance with her too. Mark seemed to be taking an awfully long time to fetch her drink. She glanced over her shoulder towards the door—and found herself looking up into a pair of cool grey eyes.

'Mind if I cut in?' he asked in a lazy drawl. Her partner offered no objection, leaving her no choice but to accede. Reluctantly she turned to him, wishing she hadn't chosen to wear a dress that gave him an excuse to let his gaze linger over the curves of her body in such an insolent way. 'You're very popular,' he remarked. 'I thought I was never going to get a look in.'

'I know a lot of people here.'

'I see. It's got nothing to do with you being the most beautiful woman in the room, then?'

Her eyes flashed coldly. 'What about Lisa?' she enquired. 'You don't think she deserves that accolade?'

He laughed mockingly. 'You know she doesn't hold a candle to you,' he murmured, letting his voice take on a husky timbre.

'How long have you known her?' Jess asked coolly, determined to maintain a distance between them.

'Oh, a couple of years on and off.'

'And how long have you been going out with her?'

He lifted one eyebrow enquiringly. 'Going out with her? What makes you think that I am?'

'Aren't you?'

He only laughed, and as the music changed to a slower beat he circled his arm around her waist and drew her closer. She put up her hands to hold him away, but as her fingertips encountered the hardness of his chest beneath the check shirt an unexpected quiver of excitement ran through her—he was all male, in a way that made her feel more vulnerable than she could ever recall feeling before.

He smiled down at her, his hypnotic gaze mesmerising her, and the warmth of his strong arms slowly melted the steel in her spine. Almost unconsciously she let him mould her body intimately to him, closing her eyes as reality drifted away. The sensuous words of the song were seducing her mind, she was drugged by the musky maleness that was invading her senses, betrayed by a weakness that was as old as Adam and Eve.

'Jezebel,' he murmured softly in her ear, making the hated name sound like a caress. 'It suits you— you could tempt a man to sell his soul.'

She wanted to drag herself away from him, but she couldn't—he was in control, and she didn't know how to defend herself. His hand had slid down to mould intimately over the base of her spine, holding her far too close for modesty, and strange, disturbing images were swirling in her brain.

'Oh, there you are, darling. So you did decide to dance with the boss after all.' Lisa's tinkling laugh slashed through the spell like a cold knife. 'He said you wouldn't like it, but I told him not to be silly. After all, even though you're his boss, you're practically my best friend.'

Jess managed a thin smile, refusing to meet Sam's eyes as Lisa firmly reclaimed him. Mark had reappeared too, jealous anger marring his handsome face. 'I've brought your drink,' he announced grumpily.

'Oh, darling, thank you,' purred Jess, sliding quickly into his arms. 'I was beginning to wonder where you'd got to.'

'The bar was packed,' he explained, slightly mollified. 'You seemed to be enjoying yourself well enough,' he added, remembering the cause of his complaint. 'Have you been dancing with him all the time I've been gone?'

'Of course not,' she assured him, forgetting to be annoyed by his possessiveness. 'I've danced with lots of people—Paul, and Stephen, and Jonathan Carey—you remember him? He went out to Hong Kong with his bank—he's been telling me all about it, it sounds marvellous. I wish I could get some contacts out there—they're building all the time.'

'Oh, don't start talking about that damn construction business again,' grumbled Mark crossly. 'Come on, let's dance.'

'Oh, no—it's much too hot,' she protested quickly, feeling a sudden revulsion against the thought of letting him hold her close again.

'Well, let's go outside for a bit of fresh air, then,' he suggested.

Jess gave in, and they squeezed their way through to the french windows, which were open to give access to the garden. The cool evening air was deliciously refreshing, and Jess breathed it in with a contented sigh. She tensed as Mark came up close behind her, and wrapped his arms around her, burying his face in the hollow of her shoulder. 'Mmm. I could eat you,' he mumbled thickly.

She moved out of his grasp. 'Roses!' she remarked, clutching at any excuse to get away from him. 'Don't they smell lovely at night?'

She climbed the stone steps to the main part of the garden, and strolled along the flagged path. Mark followed her. The fresh air seemed to have affected him rather badly, and he was stumbling a little. Jess put out her hand instinctively, and found herself supporting his whole weight. There was a gazebo nearby, with a stone bench-seat, and somehow she managed to get him into it.

'Jez!' He fell against her, breathing sickly fumes in her face. 'I'm crazy about you.' His hands were wandering up over her body, and she tried to wriggle away from him. 'No! Don't go away,' he protested. 'You always push me off. I'm as good as all the others—better, 'cause I really care about you.'

'You've a funny way of showing it,' she snapped crossly. 'Let me go.'

But he was a strong man, and alcohol had made him forget his usual gentlemanly manners. 'I want you, Jez,' he panted urgently. 'You've done nothing but mess me about . . .'

Suddenly Jess was really frightened. He had pushed her back along the seat, and was almost suffocating her beneath his weight. His fumbling hands were trying to caress her, and as she fought desperately to push him away he lost his patience. A cry of horror broke from her lips as he ripped her dress, baring the full curve of one pink-tipped breast in the silver moonlight.

Suddenly a cool voice spoke in the darkness. 'I hope I'm not interrupting anything, but I wondered if either of you needed any assistance.'

Mark swore savagely as he looked up to see a large figure leaning casually against side of the gazebo. 'What the hell has it got to do with you?' he snarled.

'Not a great deal, I agree,' drawled Sam. 'But when I hear a lady—I use the term loosely, of course—evidently in distress, I somehow can't keep from poking my nose in. Particularly when that lady happens to be my boss.'

His voice was as smooth as silk, but there was an unmistakable thread of steel in it that gave Mark pause. He rose slowly to his feet, his fists clenching and unclenching uncertainly. But a fuller appraisal of Sam's wide shoulders engendered discretion, and with a final fierce oath he shoved past Sam and vanished towards the house.

Sam shook his head pensively as he watched him go. 'Poor boy,' he mused. 'Whatever were you doing to him?'

Jess struggled to sit up, clutching at the torn strips of her dress to cover her modesty. 'What was *I* doing to *him*?' she repeated, aghast. 'What about me? Don't you think I should get a little sympathy?'

'Of course.' He hesitated, as if racking his brains for something to offer. 'Er...that bench looks rather hard.'

Jess couldn't help laughing, in spite of her embarrassment. Her hair was in disarray, her make-up streaked, her tights laddered. Sam surveyed her with lazy mockery. 'You look a mess,' he informed her.

'Thank you.'

'I'd better take you home.'

She slanted a wary glance up at him. 'Won't Lisa object to that?' she asked, a hint of sarcasm in her voice.

'Of course not,' he countered. 'After all, you're practically her best friend.' Jess didn't answer, not quite sure if his mockery was directed at herself or Lisa. 'Where's your coat?'

She told him reluctantly. 'It's in the spare room. A blue velvet jacket.'

'Velvet? I expected mink at the very least,' he teased.

'I don't wear fur,' she responded with dignity.

'I stand corrected.'

She sat shivering, waiting for him to come back with her jacket, her emotions a cauldron. Damn Mark—why did he have to put her in such an embarrassing position? And with Sam of all people! And was he really going out with Lisa, or not? Not that she cared, of course, except in so far as it might affect his loyalty to McGill Construction.

She heard his footsteps returning, and stood up quickly. She felt terribly vulnerable after that awful scene with Mark, but somehow she had to try to regain her dignity. She met his eyes boldly as he stepped into the gazebo. 'Ah, thank you,' she said, a deceptive confidence in her voice.

'Don't mention it,' he responded politely as he helped her into her jacket. They left the garden by the back gate, and walked out into the quiet street. 'I trust you won't object to riding in my old Land Rover?'

'Not at all.'

'Good. I used to have an XJ6,' he added, a hint of ironic self-mockery in his voice, 'but that went along with everything else.'

Jess looked up at him covertly from beneath her lashes. 'I suppose it must be quite difficult for you now, working for someone else when you've been your own boss,' she speculated.

'It would be,' he responded levelly, 'if I thought it was going to be for ever.'

'You intend to start your own business again one day?'

'Of course. Here we are.' He opened the passenger door of the battered old car, bowing in mocking formality. At least the seat was clean, and she climbed into it carefully. He walked round to the driver's side and slid in beside her.

She glanced along the spartan dashboard. 'What's that?' she asked, pointing to a deep graze.

'A bullet-hole,' he told her in a matter-of-fact tone. 'It came through here and missed the engine-block by inches.'

She stared at him, wondering if he was joking, but sure enough there was a small patch of metal-filler just behind his shoulder. If he was driving, it must have missed him by inches too. 'How did it happen?' she asked faintly.

'On the way out of San Marcos. A bunch of young hot-heads didn't want us to leave.'

She slanted him a glance of mocking enquiry. 'I heard you went in by plane to get your men out.'

He chuckled with laughter. 'Who told you that?'

'A friend of Lisa's.'

He shook his head, a broad grin on his face. 'It just goes to show how people will exaggerate,' he remarked. 'Where are we going, by the way?'

She gave him her address, and he turned into the Fulham Road. She was watching him from beneath her lashes, still curious to know more about him. 'So it wasn't a daring rescue then?' she asked, a trace of sarcasm in her voice.

He seemed to find this highly amusing. 'More like a very hasty withdrawal,' he drawled laconically.

Jess eyed him thoughtfully, impressed in spite of herself by his coolness. She knew that her own workers respected him enormously—it was said that he could do every job on the site as well as any one of the craftsmen.

The streets of London were deserted, and it took only a few minutes to reach the Fulham Road apartment block where Jess lived. Suddenly she felt strangely uncertain, not sure how to handle the situation. She, who was always in control—she felt as shy as a schoolgirl!

'Well—thank you for bringing me home,' she mumbled.

That faintly mocking smile had curved his mouth again. 'You're not quite home yet,' he pointed out.

'Oh, but...you don't have to come up,' she protested quickly.

'I never like to leave a job half finished,' he responded, getting out of the car and coming round to open her door.

Her legs felt weak as she stood up. This was crazy—she was his employer, for goodness' sake! He was going out with Lisa. But all she could think about was the way he had pinned her up against the car park wall the first time she had met him, and seemed so nearly ready to kiss her.

She managed a brief smile for the night porter in the entrance-hall of the block, and when the lift came she stood as far from Sam as she could. Their footsteps were silent on the deep carpet of the corridor that led to her front door. She fumbled in her bag for her key, and then turned to face him.

'Well...goodnight,' she stammered. Calmly he took the key from her hand and opened the door, propelling her firmly inside. As he closed the door behind them both and drew her into his arms she uttered a faint cry of protest. 'What...?'

'You don't expect me to kiss you goodnight outside, do you?' he asked, his grey eyes laughing down into hers.

'I don't expect you to kiss me goodnight at all,' she declared angrily, trying to pull away from him.

He overcame her resistance with ease, drawing her very close. 'Ah, then you don't know me very well,' he murmured, lowering his mouth over hers. His sensuous tongue swept languorously over the delicate inner membranes of her lips, coaxing her to yield little by little. But part of her brain still fought for sanity, and she pushed him away.

'Hadn't you better be getting back to the party?' she asked unsteadily. 'Lisa will be wondering where you are.'

'She knows where I am.'

'Oh? You asked permission, then?' she queried spitefully.

He laughed softly, shaking his head. 'I've no need to,' he answered, deliberately provocative. 'She isn't a domineering bitch like you.'

The words hurt every bit as much as he had meant them too, and he took full advantage of her momentary weakness, gathering her up in his arms again, claiming her mouth with ruthless insistence. His kiss was deep and demanding, and as he curved her body against his she felt the masculine power in him, and a warm tide of submissiveness flooded through her.

Sensing her surrender, he slid his hand inside her velvet jacket, and brushed aside the torn threads of her dress to caress the naked curve of her breast. His touch stirred a dizzying excitement in her veins, making her blood pound in her ears, drowning out any last rational thoughts. His clever fingers stroked possessively over her silken skin, teasing the ripe, tender bud of her nipple, searing her brain with incandescent heat.

He lifted his head, and gazed down into her eyes. 'I want you, Jezebel,' he murmured smokily. Her traitorous body answered for her, giving him every reason to be confident of his victory. He laughed, low in his throat. 'We'll be more comfortable in bed.'

Somehow she managed to drag herself back from the brink as she realised what he was expecting. She shook her head, her eyes wide as she stared up at him.

He frowned, puzzled by her contrariness. 'Why not?'

'Just no,' she whispered, shaking her head again. 'Please go away.'

He didn't argue: he didn't say a word. He opened the door and went out, closing it firmly behind him, leaving her leaning weakly against the wall, quivering with reaction.

CHAPTER THREE

'I'M DREADING this,' admitted Jess in a tense voice.

Fiona smiled reassuringly. 'You'll sail through it. And you look fabulous.'

'I was hoping I looked businesslike,' Jess told her wryly. This was to be her first meeting with all the senior engineering staff of McGill Construction. She had met them all individually, but the thought of confronting their combined experience and technical skill was daunting.

She had chosen to wear a very masculine-styled suit, grey pin-striped worsted, severely cut, with a crisp white shirt and a thin bow-tie of emerald green ribbon. She had put her hair up, too, but the reaction she had got from everyone from the car park attendant to Bill, her cost analyst, told her that far from disguising her sexuality, as she had intended, she had succeeded only in emphasising it.

'Don't worry,' urged Fiona. 'You'll have them eating out of your hand. Now, these are the computer print-outs of the network-schedules on all the current contracts, including the TDC contract.'

'We haven't got it yet.'

'Sam thinks we've got an excellent chance,' said Fiona in a tone that implied that Sam's confidence was all that was needed.

'I hope he's right,' sighed Jess. 'The Homes division is doing very badly, and Roads aren't much better.'

'There could be that council renovation scheme coming up soon,' Fiona reminded her. 'That should be very worthwhile.'

'But the competition's pretty fierce. Times are bad for everyone.' She scanned through the network-schedules. 'And look—we're behind on nearly every contract—some of them badly. We're never going to complete the Sports Complex project on time.'

Fiona glanced at the sheet, and nodded. 'Angus was a little over-optimistic on that one—Sam told him so at the time, but he wouldn't listen.'

Jess smiled ruefully. 'Yes—but you know who everyone's going to say messed it up, don't you? Yours truly. Just because I'm a woman, and their great big male egos can't bear to think of a woman muscling in on something so all-fired macho as the building industry.'

Fiona laughed. 'Oh, I have to admit you're in for an uphill struggle,' she conceded. 'But you don't mind that, do you?'

Jess's delicate mouth thinned into a smile of grim determination. 'Not a bit,' she declared fiercely. 'I'll show 'em.'

'That's the spirit. Ah, I think I hear the first arrivals.'

Fiona hurried out to her own office to see who was there, and Jess took a deep breath, steadying herself for the coming ordeal. It wasn't only the business side she was dreading. It would be the first time she had seen Sam since the night of Lisa's party. How would he behave towards her? Would he attempt to exploit what had happened to gain for himself some sort of advantage? It was with the utmost trepidation that she watched the door open.

But Sam was not among the first to arrive. Bill French had come along from his own office with Bernard, the Purchasing Manger, and Jack, the head of the ailing Homes division. They were locked in a heated debate about drainage that Jess couldn't follow at all. When Peter and Carl from Roads arrived, they too chipped into the discussion.

'It's all a matter of compaction,' insisted Jack. 'There's too much clay in the soil—your suggestion just wouldn't work.'

'That's right,' chimed in Peter. 'We had a very similar problem last year on that Kent Council contract. You must remember, Bill.'

'So what did you do?' asked Jack.

Jess leaned forward, eager to learn. She didn't understand the technical jargon at all, but when Carl drew a diagram for her on the back of one of the network-schedules she found that it became fascinatingly clear. 'Oh, I see. So it works a bit like a raft?' she queried, studying the drawing.

'Exactly. You absorb the stresses from here...'

Without looking up, Jess knew that Sam had come into the room. The rest of Carl's detailed explanation was lost on her. He was talking quietly to one of the senior quantity surveyors, and Jess could sense that he was totally at ease, sharing none of her apprehension.

She made herself look up and smile at them all. It was a model-girl smile, put on for the cameras and masking everything that was inside. 'Well, gentlemen,' she began coolly, 'it seems that everyone is here now. Shall we make a start?'

A murmur of assent went round the room. They took their seats with an air of falling into long-accustomed habit—even Fiona, sitting beside her, pencil and shorthand book at the ready, seemed part of that old order, from which Jess felt herself excluded.

'I'd like to thank you all for coming,' she went on. 'We've a lot of business to get through, not all of it good. I will do my best to understand the technical side of things, but I hope you'll bear with me if I seem a bit thick at times.' They laughed politely—all except Sam, who was glancing through the schedules.

'Perhaps we'd better get the really bad news out of the way first, Jack. What's happening in your division?'

'We're virtually at a standstill,' Jack admitted glumly. 'There's absolutely nothing in the pipeline. And the problem is, the men know they're going to get laid off, and that's making completion on the current contracts even more difficult.'

Carl shook his head. 'It'd be a shame to lay off any of your men—they're a damn fine team.'

Jack shrugged. 'I know that. I've worked with some of those chaps for years. But none of the councils are building much at the moment, and the private side isn't much better.'

'Will we be able to use some of them on the TDC contract if we get it?' asked Bill.

Sam glanced up. 'Possibly—if we get the contract.'

'Any reason why we shouldn't?' someone asked.

'About a dozen, and all of them our main competitors,' remarked Sam laconically.

'I don't see how they can undercut us,' put in Bill. 'Those costings were as tight as a...as tight as they could be,' he corrected himself swiftly, with an embarrassed glance at Jess.

Again Jess felt uncomfortable, an intruder. These men were used to speaking in the vernacular, and they were trying to guard their tongues in deference to her presence. Sam had barely glanced in her direction— although he hadn't actually ignored her either. He seemed indifferent to her, and after the way he had treated her on their previous meetings she found that difficult to handle.

The meeting wore on. Each division told the same gloomy story—a worrying shortage of future contracts, discontent among the work-force, projects falling behind schedule. Even to a novice like Jess, it was clear that the three problems were interrelated.

She was learning fast. Jack had explained to her the principles of Gantt charts, and she had watched in fascination as a computer had plotted a network-schedule, graphically representing the whole programme for the construction of a building. And Bill was initiating her into the secrets of time-cost curves and crash-points.

Now she had to go out and hustle for contracts, as Angus had done. She had to convince people that McGill Construction was as good as it had ever been, that they could still be relied on for quality workmanship without unnecessary delays.

At last the meeting came to an end. 'Well, I think that's everything,' she was able to say with a tinge of relief. 'Once again, thank you all for coming. I would like to come out to each of the sites to see for myself what we are doing, and to learn as much as I can about this business. Fiona, perhaps you could check my diary, and make the arrangements.'

'Of course.'

Jess smiled her farewells as the men stood up and took their leave, following Fiona into the outer office. All but Sam. Jess turned all her attention to sorting through the notes on her desk, trying hard to ignore him. He was still sitting as he had sat all through the meeting, totally relaxed, his long legs stretched in front of him, but now he was watching her with that steady gaze that she found so disconcerting.

'You're going to have to prune your head-office staff, you know,' he remarked.

She lifted her eyes slowly to his face, and regarded him as if he were some unpleasant sort of insect that had no right to be in her nice office. 'I beg your pardon?'

He rose and came over to lean his hands on the desk, towering over her. 'You've too many men in the drawing-office, too many engineers with nothing to do,' he said. 'Maybe things'll pick up again in a year or two, but you can't go on paying salaries for men to sit idle.'

'Oh, yes? And how do you suggest I tell them that their services are no longer required?' she asked, all the more annoyed because she had reluctantly been thinking the same thing herself.

Sam shrugged his wide shoulders. 'If you're going to run this firm, you've got to be prepared to take a few tough decisions. No one expects charity.'

Jess's eyes were as cold as the North Atlantic as she looked up at him. 'Indeed? And does that include you?'

He laughed mockingly. 'Oh, I wouldn't have to look far to get another job,' he taunted. 'Bob Carter would take me on just like that.' He snapped his fingers.

Jess felt a chill. 'Lisa's father?'

He nodded.

'Well, if you want to work for him, perhaps you'd better give me your resignation,' she challenged, determined not to be blackmailed.

'Oh, I'll give you a fair chance,' he responded evenly. 'I owe Angus that much.'

Jess couldn't think of an answer. She couldn't afford to let Sam go, much as her pride urged her to tell him what he could do with his favours. She injected several degrees of frost into her voice as she said, 'Good afternoon, Mr Ryder.'

'What are you going to do about the redundancies?'

'Nothing.'

'You're a fool.'

She didn't trouble to look up from the notes she was transcribing. 'Good afternoon, Mr Ryder.'

'And I wouldn't recommend you to visit the sites,' he added in a grim tone.

'Oh?'

'I told you before—a lot of the men don't like working for a woman. It'll only serve to remind them. You've got labour problems already. If I were you, I'd wait a while, until they've had a chance to get used to the idea.'

She looked up at him coldly. 'Do you have any more suggestions?' she enquired in glacial accents.

'Several. But you're so damned obstinate, I don't suppose you'll listen, so I'll save my breath until you've learned your lesson.'

'Thank you, Mr Ryder,' Jess responded tartly. 'Good afternoon.'

She heard again that mocking laughter as he strolled towards the door. 'Just remember one thing,' he remarked over his shoulder.

She lifted one finely arched eyebrow in cool enquiry.

'You need me a lot more than I need you. Good afternoon, Jezebel.'

Before she could think of a suitable parting shot he was gone, closing the door firmly behind him. She picked up a paper-clip, twisting it between tense fingers until it snapped. He was right, damn him. She might be the boss, but he was the one in control.

By the time she had made a couple of site-visits she began to realise that Sam had been right about the men's attitude towards her. Even though she had dressed in what she thought were sensible clothes—tobacco-brown corduroy trousers tucked into the tops of her tan leather boots, and a smart tweed hacking-jacket—she had been met by a chorus of loud and derisory wolf-whistles wherever she went.

After a couple of days spent picking her way around puddles and between piles of sand she had settled for a pair of inelegant wellington boots and a thick sweater. But wearing the right clothes gave her no entrée to this world—everywhere she met suspicion and hostility. At times she was tempted to abandon her tour of inspection, but she was determined not to give in to this silent male conspiracy.

It was that dimension which made this job so difficult. She had thought that her experience in running the design agency would have been more of a help—after all, she was no more a graphic artist than she was a civil engineer. It had been her role to bring together customer and technician—as now.

She had started the agency with her own money, saved from her model earnings. From small beginnings it had been doing quite well—until a big American firm had decided that the logo she had had designed for one of her customers was too much like their own. They had sued the customer—and they could afford to hire one of the country's leading barristers to do it—and the customer in turn had sued her. Losing had been expensive in terms of both her money and her reputation.

Getting started a second time had been difficult, but she would have done it—if Angus hadn't died and left the future of McGill Construction in her hands. Poor Angus—he had been barely fifty. He must have thought he had many years to arrange his affairs.

It would be easy enough to sell out—she had had several good offers. But then McGill Construction would become just an anonymous adjunct of some big corporation. Angus had resisted that all his life. No—she had to keep the firm going. Once she had found her feet, won a few contracts, people would begin to see that she was as good as any man.

She was to meet Sam again at the Sports Complex. It was a prestige project, a huge development incorporating a swimming-pool, indoor tennis-courts, squash-courts, dance studio and gymnasium. But it had run into problems almost from the beginning, and now every day that passed was eating into the profit margin, almost to the point where they were going to start losing money on it.

Jess had studied every paper that related to the contract, and her quick mind was already picking up a great deal of useful knowledge. But she guessed that Sam would make mincemeat of her, and she wasn't looking forward to their meeting at all.

She set off early to drive up the motorway. It was a misty morning, but as the sun rose the mist lifted over a mellow autumn landscape of russet and gold, fading hill by hill into the distance. It was a little after ten o'clock as she spotted the sign announcing 'McGill Construction—Site Traffic Only'.

It was a lovely building, behind the cage of scaffolding that still surrounded it. Unashamedly modern, prisms of bronzed glass winked back at the weak October sun. Jess drew her car to a halt in front of the site office and climbed out, gazing up admiringly at the shining cliff above her.

'Beautiful bitch, isn't she?'

Jess turned quickly. Sam was standing in the doorway with another man. The other man was looking up at the building, but Sam's steel-grey eyes rested insolently on Jess's neat figure. She shot him a fulminating glare, but met only that mocking smile.

'She's certainly given us some problems,' the other man agreed innocently.

'Jess, this is Fred Upshaw, the Site Manager,' Sam introduced her.

Jess had learned from her earlier encounters with her senior site staff that a certain amount of old-fashioned formality was expected. She came forward with a warm smile, extending her hand. 'Good morning, Mr Upshaw,' she said. 'How near are we to completion here now?'

Fred shrugged non-committally. 'We've had a lot of problems with suppliers,' he said. 'And I'm afraid Angus's insistence on laying off labourers if they weren't needed for a day or two hasn't helped morale here on site. But things are progressing more smoothly now—I don't think we'll have too many more problems.'

'Good. Can I have a look inside the building?'

'Of course. Come and get a hard-hat,' he invited.

He turned to step back into the site-hut, but in the doorway he paused. Glancing past him, Jess saw what had embarrassed him. Pinned to the wall above the cluttered desk was one of the 'Jezebel' ads, torn from a magazine.

She felt her cheeks flush scarlet. It was a long time since she had seen any of those pictures, and she had half forgotten how bad they were. And though she had known that they had been popular as pin-ups she had only ever seen them in magazines. Somehow it seemed far more sordid, tacked up there on the wall. She felt a surge of humiliation. How could she command any respect, when every time the men stepped into the office they could feast their eyes on that?

'I'm terribly sorry, Miss McGill,' Fred protested quickly. 'I thought it had been taken down.'

She glanced up at Sam. His expression was bland, and humiliation was replaced by cold fury. He had put it there, to embarrass her. Pride lifted her head as she said coolly, 'That's quite all right, Mr Upshaw. Think nothing of it—I'm sure I don't.'

Sam studied the picture as if seeing it for the first time. 'Mmm,' he taunted softly, 'you're very photogenic.'

'Thank you,' she responded with a smile as bland as his own, and turned to accept a safety-helmet from Fred.

It was a strange, almost surreal world inside the shell of the building: bare steel girders, and cascades of electric cable, and a vast echoing cavern where the upper floors had not yet been laid. The south-facing glass wall which Jess had seen from the outside gave a sort of golden Mediterranean glow to the atmosphere.

Sam turned to help her climb up on to the narrow cat-walk running around the ground-floor level, and took the opportunity to subject her to another appraising scrutiny. 'I can't say I like your outfit,' he remarked provokingly.

'It isn't intended to attract the likes of you,' she retorted, favouring him with her frostiest look. 'It's just practical.'

'I'd much rather see you wearing what you've got on in that picture,' he murmured, stopping unexpectedly so that she found herself suddenly far too close to him. 'For what I've got in mind that's *much* more practical.'

She stepped back hastily, and almost fell off the cat-walk. He reached out swiftly and caught her. 'Careful—watch your step,' he chided, a mocking gleam in his eyes.

She shot him a fulminating glare, but he seemed maddeningly impervious to her anger. Turning him an aloof shoulder, she moved ahead of him to walk with Fred Upshaw, who treated her with a proper degree of courtesy, answering all her questions with patience. But all the time she was aware of Sam strolling along behind them, his hands deep in the pockets of his mud-splashed jeans. It made her feel self-conscious, knowing that he was watching her— knowing that he was seeing the woman in that picture, not the boss of McGill Construction.

Suddenly one of the workmen came up to them. 'Sam, I'm sorry, but these sealing-junctions still aren't right. The angles are out on at least a dozen of them.'

'I'll come and look,' he agreed at once. 'Excuse me,' he added to Jess.

'Where are you going?'

'Up to the roof.'

'I'd like to see.'

'Well, you can't. The only way to get up there at the moment is by the scaffolding.'

'That doesn't bother me. I'm not afraid of heights,' she responded firmly.

'I don't care. You're not coming up on the scaf- folding—it gets very windy here, and it's dangerous if you don't know what you're doing.'

'Mr Ryder, may I remind you that I am the boss of McGill Construction?'

'Did Angus ever let you up on scaffolding?'

'No, but . . .'

'Then neither will I,' he concluded with an air of finality.

She hurried after him as he walked outside to where the cage rested on the muddy ground. 'I'm warning you, Sam...'

He turned on her abruptly. 'And I'm warning you. You may own the company, but I'm responsible for what goes on out here on the sites. And we've got enough problems, without you stamping your foot and demanding your own way like a spoilt child.'

She stared at him, momentarily stunned, and he stepped into the cage and slammed the gate shut behind him. He pulled the lever, and the cage began to ascend on its ropes. Jess watched in cold fury. As soon as he had stepped out, and vanished round the corner of the building, she summoned the cage, and stepped inside.

It rose slowly, buffeted by the wind as it reached the second storey. It jerked to a halt and she stepped out on to the rough planking. It was harder to stay on her feet than she had thought. Stacks of breeze-blocks obstructed her path, and she moved round them cautiously, clinging to the poles of the scaffolding to haul herself along.

As she turned the corner, a sudden fierce gust almost knocked her over. She struggled to regain her balance, stumbling over a cement-trowel. With a loud clatter it vanished over the edge. She stared down guiltily, her heart pounding with shock as she realised how dangerous it could have been if someone had been walking past below.

A steel hand closed round her arm. 'You stupid idiot. You could have killed someone. I ought to put you over my knee!'

The knowledge that he was all too right served only to put her on the defensive. She glared up in angry defiance into those cold grey eyes. 'Take your hands off me, you big ape!' she demanded furiously. 'How dare you speak to me like that?'

His mouth set into a grim line. Without a word he hustled her along the scaffolding towards the cage. She tried to twist free of him, but he held her in a grip that was almost savage. 'Let me go, damn you,' she hissed, aware of a dozen faces uplifted below them.

He hauled her into the cage and closed the gate, and pulled the lever to take them to the ground. More men had stopped work, and were watching the developing scene with interest. Rage and humiliation boiled inside her, sweeping aside all rational thought. She struck out at him with a wildly swinging fist. 'You're fired!' she cried, her voice choked with angry tears.

He parried the blow with ease. 'That suits me fine,' he rasped, his face inches above hers. 'And while I'm at it, I might as well be hung for a sheep as a lamb.'

She was trapped in his arms, her body crushed against him as he captured her mouth in a kiss that was pure savagery. She fought to resist him, but her mercurial spirit ignited, and she began to respond. There was no gentleness in him as he plundered the sweetest depths of her mouth, demanding nothing less than total surrender. Her blood was racing, her spine melting into his embrace. He was no longer imprisoning her—she had lifted her arms to wrap them around his neck, offering him everything he asked.

The cage came to rest on the ground, and he lifted his head. She stared up into his eyes, stunned by the turmoil that was raging inside her. Suddenly she became aware of the sound of laughing and cheering, and stared around in horror. Every man on the site must have stopped work and come to watch the fun!

Sam's mouth curled into something close to a sneer. 'There—now I'm well and truly fired, aren't I?' he mocked.

'Get away from me,' she spat. 'I hate you!'

He laughed tauntingly. 'What a little hell-cat you are, Jezebel. But you're going to regret this morning's work. I told you—you need me far more than I need you.'

'I don't need you,' she shouted as he stepped out of the cage. The crowd parted to let him through. 'Go and try your cave-man tactics on Lisa. I'm sure she'll be much more impressed.'

His shoulders shook with laughter. 'Perhaps I will,' he conceded musingly as he walked away. 'Yes, maybe I might just do that.'

She stared after him, her fury ebbing away into a tide of embarrassment before that sea of grinning faces. But pride lifted her head, and with a brisk step she marched over to her car and got in, and gunned the engine fiercely to spin away at top speed.

CHAPTER FOUR

IT was soon evident that without Sam, things were beginning to go wrong. Little things at first—a special price he had negotiated for bitumen sealing strips was not available on the repeat order. But soon it was worse—the expected TDC contract failed to materialise, and labour problems on the Sports Complex site were getting out of hand.

Meanwhile Sam and Lisa were seen everywhere together. Everyone agreed they made a charming couple, and Jess's society smile was becoming increasingly brittle. Dining out with Mark—having forgiven him for his reprehensible behaviour at Lisa's party—she came face to face with them.

It was a surprise to see Sam in a dinner-jacket. Oddly, it suited him remarkably well, moulding his wide shoulders to perfection; but somehow the formal elegance of the outfit did nothing to detract from that air of raw masculine power that emanated from him—or maybe it was the casual self-assurance in his stride as he walked through the exclusive restaurant. Whatever it was, every female in the room seemed to sense it, and Lisa positively simpered with pride as she clung to his arm.

'Jez! How lovely to see you,' she gushed as they came up to their table. 'You look simply fabulous, doesn't she, Sam?'

'As always.'

Jess's teeth were on edge behind her smile. 'Thank you,' she murmured conventionally.

'It seems simply ages since I've seen you,' Lisa rushed on. 'But then we haven't been out a great deal, have we, Sam?' The arch look she slanted up at him from beneath her lashes left no doubt that they hadn't been staying in to play Scrabble. 'Did you know Sam's working for Daddy now?' Lisa added, unable to keep the gleam of triumph from her eyes.

'Yes, I did know,' Jess responded coolly.

'They get on ever so well, don't you, Sam? I've never known Daddy take to anyone quite so easily.'

'How fortunate.' The acid on Jess's tongue rivalled the vinaigrette on her salad.

'Oh, our table's ready. Must dash. Bye-ee! See you later.' Lisa twiddled her fingers in a sweet little wave, and tugged on Sam's arm. 'Come along, darling,' she urged.

He looked down on Jess and Mark from his lofty height, that faintly mocking smile on his hard mouth. He was fully aware of the hostility with which they both regarded him, but it didn't seem to trouble him in the least. 'Bye-ee,' he murmured. Once again Jess was startled by the way he seemed to be deriding Lisa's affected mannerisms—and yet if he found her so silly, why was he going out with her?

'I really don't know what Lisa sees in that creep,' Mark hissed as soon as they were out of earshot.

'He isn't a creep!' protested Jess without thinking. 'At least . . .well, I can't say I like him, but you could hardly call him a creep.'

'Well, maybe creep is the wrong word,' conceded Mark grumpily. 'But he thinks he's the greatest thing since sliced bread.'

Jess found herself unable to disagree with that. All through the rest of the meal she was aware of the other couple across the room. Lisa seemed to be entertaining Sam with a ceaseless flow of chatter, to which he was responding with that smile of slightly mocking amusement. But now and then Jess would sense that he was watching her, and her eyes would be drawn to his as if by a force stronger than gravity itself.

He seemed to be taunting her, reminding her of the truth of what he had said—she needed him more than he needed her. He was doing very nicely, working for Bob Carter and dating his daughter, while McGill Construction was floundering. As he lifted his wineglass to his lips he saluted her sardonically, and she felt her cheeks flush faintly pink, vividly remembering what had happened the last time they had met.

Her nerves stretched to breaking-point, she tried to escape for a few minutes by retreating to the ladies' room, but Lisa found her there. She was bubbling with vivacity, as eager to talk about Sam as Jess was to forget his very existence. 'Oh, Jez,' she burbled, 'you do forgive me, don't you?'

'Forgive you? Whatever for?'

'For stealing Sam. Daddy was *so* pleased when he agreed to come and work for him, but I did feel just a teensy bit guilty for persuading him when he was working for you.'

'Did you, Lisa?' enquired Jess coolly. 'I don't see why you should.'

Lisa giggled. 'Well, yes, I suppose all's fair in love and war, as they say. But you're my friend, and I know some people might not think that's important, but I do.'

Jess concentrated on combing her wild curls into some semblance of order. There were times when she could have cheerfully wrung Lisa's sweet little neck.

Lisa was combing her own silken blonde locks, her sapphire blue eyes dreamy. 'If I tell you a secret, do you promise not to tell anyone else?' she asked. Jess merely lifted an enquiring eyebrow. 'Sam and I are going to get married,' she confided happily.

Not by a quaver did Jess betray the sudden thud of her heart. Marry Lisa? What on earth did he see in her? Surely he couldn't be in love with her—he had too much sense. As levelly as she could, she said, 'Really? Congratulations. When's the happy day?'

'Oh, nothing's fixed up for definite yet,' Lisa answered breezily, 'but we've got an understanding.'

An 'understanding'? What exactly did that mean? Was Lisa telling the truth? She certainly wasn't going to gratify her by appearing unduly interested. She dropped her comb back into her handbag, and gave Lisa a bland smile. 'How nice,' she murmured, matching the sugary tone. 'Well, I must be off. Bye-ee.'

She felt Sam's eyes on her the minute she walked back into the restaurant. She moved with long-legged grace between the tables, conscious of the way the subtly-clinging cut of her black dress moulded her svelte figure. But try as she might to ignore that level gaze, he seemed to draw her towards him with a compulsion she couldn't resist. That faint smile was hovering over his mouth, as if he was fully aware of the strange effect he had on her.

Vainly she sought for something clever to say, but the only thing she could think of was, 'So you decided to take up Bob Carter's offer, then?'

'I needed a job.'

'I fully expected you to sue me for unfair dismissal,' she taunted.

He lifted one eyebrow in amused enquiry. 'Did you? Why should you think I'd want to do that?'

'You could have won substantial damages,' she pointed out.

'But I'm not interested in a confrontation with you. I prefer a quiet life,' he answered.

She eyed him doubtfully. There was nothing in the strong line of his jaw that suggested a passive disposition. As she hesitated, trying to think of a smart retort, his glance moved past her, and his eyes warmed into a special intimate smile for Lisa as she approached. Jess felt herself driven into retreat, but she lifted her head proudly. 'Well, I'll wish you luck then,' she said.

Sam spared her barely a glance as he responded absently, 'Thank you.'

The image of that smile he had given Lisa was burning inside her head as she made her way back to her own table. Maybe he really was going to marry her. But surely he could see through that sugary façade to the selfish, manipulative creature beneath? Or maybe he couldn't—Lisa had played out her role for so long she was word perfect. He probably thought he was getting a sweet, submissive little wife. Well, if he was that easily fooled, she thought vengefully, it served him right.

Mark's petulant voice cut across her thoughts. 'What were you chatting to *him* about then?' he demanded as she sat down.

'Oh, nothing much. Have you finished your coffee? I don't want a late night—I've got an early meeting tomorrow.'

A frown spoiled Mark's handsome face. 'That's all that's important to you now, isn't it?' he complained. 'Work, work and more work. You're the last person I ever thought would turn out that way.'

'It just goes to show how little you ever knew me then, doesn't it?' she snapped. Sometimes she wondered why she ever bothered to go out with Mark.

She had promoted Jack Hargreaves, from the Homes Division, to Sam's old job, but though he was an experienced engineer he wasn't an unqualified success as a trouble-shooter. He didn't have Sam's knack for dealing with the men. Another labour dispute had stopped work on the Sports Complex, the Homes Division was idle, and her Chief Accountant was making warning noises.

But what could she do? It seemed as though no one was prepared to give her a chance. McGill Construction hadn't won a single contract since she had taken over. It was as Sam had warned her—doors were being closed against her, just because she was a woman. Even among Angus's old friends, on whose loyalty she had hoped to rely, she found the same prejudice.

'I heard you were trying to keep the firm going by yourself. I don't know who's advising you, but I have to say I don't think you're taking the wisest course.'

Jess smiled thinly. Her lunch date was the senior partner in one of the top architectural practices in the country. 'It was my own decision, Uncle Charles, and I'm determined to make a go of it,' she told him firmly.

'But why? Surely you must have had offers?'

'I've had several.'

Charles shook his head. 'Listen, lassie, the construction industry isn't the place for a woman,' he said earnestly.

'Why not?'

'Why not? Well, I mean . . .' He spread his hands, as if the answer was self-evident.

'Look, Uncle Charles,' urged Jess, leaning forward, her eyes pleading, 'all I need is a chance to prove that McGill Construction can still do as good a job as ever. Something small—like that new telephone exchange building.'

A look of alarm came into Charles's eyes. 'What telephone exchange?' he queried guardedly.

'Oh, Uncle Charles, I know you're working on it,' she smiled. 'You told Angus about it months ago—he was going to tender for it.'

'I don't know who's going to be asked to tender,' he protested defensively.

'But you'll have some influence, won't you? Please, Uncle Charles, all I'm asking is that you put in a good word for me.'

Charles shook his head apologetically. 'I can't stake my reputation by recommending you,' he protested.

'What if you can't complete on time? It's going to be a damn inconvenience for the customer, and liquidated damages won't compensate for that, you know.'

'I can meet any conditions that are laid down,' she asserted confidently.

'What if you run into labour problems? What if suppliers let you down?'

'That can happen to anyone. I can deal with it.'

'I'm sorry, Jess. I'd like to help you. Maybe if something else comes up...' The disappointment in her face silenced him. 'It's a pity you let Bob Carter poach Sam Ryder from you.'

'He didn't poach him,' countered Jess tensely. 'I fired him.'

'You fired him? What on earth possessed you to do a damn fool thing like that?'

'We quarrelled.'

Charles snorted impatiently. 'Well, if you take my advice, you'll do your damnedest to persuade him to come back. That is, if you want to have any hope of staying in business.'

'Even if I wanted him back, which I don't,' responded Jess, controlling her feelings with some difficulty, 'I very much doubt he'd want to come. He seems perfectly happy working for Bob.'

'Rubbish. That cowboy—Ryder won't like working for him. He likes to see a job done properly, not corners cut to save a few pence.'

'Anyway, I don't need Sam,' Jess asserted. 'Jack Hargreaves is my chief engineer now.'

'Hargreaves?' Charles shook his head. 'He's good enough at his job, but if you want a ramrod you want

Sam Ryder. He's the best in the business—that's why Angus hired him.'

'He may be the best, but I don't want him working for me. He...he just isn't the sort of person I like.'

A gleam lit Charles's eyes. 'There!' he declared in triumph. 'That's exactly what I mean. Women are no good in a tough business like this. Far too emotional.'

'I will *not* negotiate with a gun held to my head,' Jess snapped furiously down the phone.

'I'm sorry, Miss McGill,' came Jack's plain voice from the Sports Complex site. 'The men just won't go back to work until the completion bonuses are agreed.'

'If they don't go back to work, there won't be any bonuses.'

'I can't tell them that,' he protested. 'There'd be an uproar.'

'Why did they have to down tools now?' wailed Jess. 'There's only a couple of days' work left. We could still complete within the time limit if they'd only co-operate.'

'I'm doing my best, Miss McGill. It isn't easy.'

'Shall I come up there myself?'

There was a momentary hesitation. 'With all due respect, Miss McGill,' came the careful reply, 'I don't think that would be a very good idea.'

'Why not?'

'There's a lot of bad talk,' he explained with difficulty. 'Your presence would only...well, aggravate the situation.'

'Then what can I do?'

'Miss McGill, I don't suppose there's any chance...I mean, I know you fired him once, but...'

'You think I should ask Sam to come back?' she queried glumly.

'Well...yes, to be honest, I do. If he could be persuaded. The men think an awful lot of him. And...well, I was thinking maybe it's time I was retiring. This job isn't really my cup of tea. Mary and I have seen a nice little cottage down Edenbridge way, and...well, you know...'

Jess sighed. 'I'll think about it, Jack,' she promised. 'In the meantime, just do what you can.'

She put down the phone, and went over to stare out of the window at the streaming traffic below. It was raining steadily, drumming on the window with a melancholy rhythm, and the sky was grey and heavy. It seemed as though it had always been November.

Jack's phone call really was the last straw. In the three months since she had taken over control of the company, she hadn't managed to secure one big contract. Oh, there was a steady trickle of sub-contracting work, but it wasn't enough to meet their overheads.

Part of the problem, she was realising, was that the firm was now top-heavy. Angus had built it in the days of the construction boom, and when recession had come he hadn't been prepared to make compromises. So now she was paying salaries to too many highly qualified technical staff who now had nothing to do but read the situations vacant columns.

Sam had been right—there would have to be redundancies. She went back to her desk, and dropped her head into her hands. There seemed to be no end to the problems. The bill from the Inland Revenue for Capital Transfer Tax on Angus's death was going to drain all the money he had left her beyond the firm and the Surrey house.

She had decided at last to sell the house, but she had had to try three estate agents before she could find one willing to take it on to his books. 'There's a glut of that sort of property on the market at the moment,' she had been told repeatedly, and it didn't look as if she would get anything like the price she had wanted for it.

The strain was taking its toll of her physically as well as mentally. She was eating on the run, snatching a sandwich or a yogurt at her desk in an odd moment, and at night her head was so full of figures and dates that she couldn't relax enough to fall asleep. She was thinner than in her modelling days, her sea-green eyes over-bright in her delicately structured face.

Jack's words echoed in her mind—Uncle Charles had said the same thing, and she knew it was murmured around the costing section and the drawing office. She needed Sam. No one else commanded the respect in the industry that could restore confidence in McGill Construction. She was going to have to swallow her pride, and ask him to come back. If he would come. He seemed perfectly happy with the situation as it was at the moment. Every time she saw him with Lisa . . .

That thought was enough to steel her resolve. She pulled open a drawer of her desk, and pulled out a sheet of writing-paper.

She didn't really expect a response to her letter—she had kept it a secret, even from Fiona. But at the exact time she had asked him to come up to the office to 'talk things over' Fiona's surprised face appeared round the door. 'Jessica—Sam Ryder's here,' she announced in a bemused tone.

Jess forced herself to maintain a calm façade, though her heart was racing. 'Thank you, Fiona. Please show him in,' she requested, keeping her voice level.

He came in with that long, lazy stride, his grey eyes hard and mocking. Jess had chosen to wear a severely styled dress of navy-blue wool, but the way he let his gaze slide over her made her feel instantly on edge. Damn the man; he had a way of reminding her, every time he looked at her, of those dreadful 'Jezebel' pictures. He didn't even have to say anything—his thoughts were plain in his eyes.

But she wasn't going to let him put her on the defensive—that would just make her lose her temper. 'Thank you for coming, Sam,' she said in a voice as cool as she could manage.

'How could I possibly resist?' he drawled laconically as he sank his large frame into one of her office chairs. 'I'm curious to learn what's made you change your tune so quickly.'

Jess took a steadying breath. 'I realised that I had been a little hasty,' she began, reciting a carefully prepared speech. 'I know I have a great deal to learn about the construction industry, but one of the things I've learnt already is that you're one of the best engineers in the country—and I want the best working for me.'

He grinned tauntingly. 'You mean you're in deep trouble, and you want me to haul you out,' he countered.

She inclined her head in minimal assent. 'Things haven't been going too well,' she conceded.

'I told you months ago that you were going to fall flat on your face,' he reminded her maddeningly.

'So you did,' she responded, her voice sharp with tension.

'You'd rather I lied to you, and told you you're doing a grand job? I don't think that's why you asked me to come up here.'

'No, of course not, but... Oh, I'm not going to argue with you—you're perfectly right, of course. I have made a bit of a mess of things so far.' She laughed weakly, resenting his air of unbreachable self-assurance. 'So, I'm offering you your old job back. On better terms, of course. What do you think?'

He leaned back lazily in his seat, laughing as he shook his head. 'Why would I want my old job back?' he queried. 'I've got a very good one at the moment.'

'You enjoy working for Bob Carter?' He shrugged his wide shoulders in cool indifference. 'You can't have much autonomy.'

'That's true enough.'

'I wouldn't have thought you were the type of man to put up with that,' she taunted.

He grinned, untroubled by her attempt to goad him. 'I don't recall that I had a great deal of autonomy at McGill,' he reminded her, an ironic inflection in his voice.

She inclined her head in assent. 'My father was rather inclined to be despotic,' she agreed.

'Your father was an unsheared lamb compared to you,' he countered in dry amusement.

She couldn't help smiling. 'I don't recall that you were exactly intimidated,' she remarked.

'No—just infuriated.'

'You could put that down to my inexperience?' she suggested.

That mocking laughter lit his eyes. 'You're the last woman I'd call inexperienced,' he drawled sardonically.

Jess felt her temperature rising. 'I meant experience in the construction industry,' she informed him tersely.

'Ah!' He nodded, enlightened.

Jess's hands were shaking, and she dropped them from the desk into her lap. He always made her so angry, with his slanting references to her 'Jezebel' image. But then he was far from being the only one who believed that the image was the reality. With an effort of will she brought her emotions under control. 'Sam, I asked you up here to discuss terms. I wouldn't have wasted your time or mine if I hadn't thought we could find scope for an agreement. I'm prepared to offer you a great deal.'

'Really?'

'You'd be virtually in complete control. I wouldn't interfere.'

'You'd just sit back and let me make you a tidy profit.'

'You'd have a share of the profits too—a good share.'

'Very generous. But the answer's still no.'

He spoke with an air of finality that smote heavily on Jess's heart, but she wasn't ready to give up yet. 'Look, Sam,' she said, instilling every ounce of genuine sincerity into her eyes, 'it wouldn't be like it was before, I promise. I know I'm inclined to be a little hasty at times...' He laughed drily. 'OK, I'm a hot-tempered bitch,' she amended. He nodded agreement. 'But I need you back. You can have things your own way—I'm virtually offering you a partnership.'

'Bob Carter is offering me a lot more than that,' he countered in a mocking drawl.

'More than a partnership? But...'

'I could own the whole company one day.' Jess stared at him blankly. 'The only hitch is that I have to marry the boss's daughter.'

Jess's heart thumped, taking her breath away. 'You'd marry Lisa to get control of Bob's business when she inherits?' she gasped, appalled.

He nodded, his eyes betraying not a flicker of emotion. 'Why not? I'd say it's a pretty good career move.'

Jess rose to her feet, and moved across to stare blindly out of the window. It had grown dark while they had been talking, and the traffic weaving around the giant roundabout had an unreal, fairground dazzle that made her feel giddy.

He really was going to marry Lisa! No... He couldn't... She couldn't let that happen! Abruptly she turned back to face him, and her voice echoed strangely in her own ears as she blurted out without giving herself time for second thoughts, 'Why marry the boss's daughter, when you can marry the boss?'

The room rang with the sound of his laughter. Jess glared at him in growing fury. Her words had been a last desperate throw, the only way she could think of to avoid the disaster of him marrying Lisa, and his derision cut her to the quick.

'Let me get this straight,' he managed to say amid peals of mirth. 'Was that a proposal?'

'Yes, it was, damn you,' she snapped furiously. 'I'd do anything to save McGill Construction—even marry you!'

'Put like that, how can I refuse?' he drawled with a mocking smile.

'Well, you needn't keep laughing about it,' she snarled. 'You can just forget I ever said it.'

'But I've accepted.'

Jess had never fainted in her life, but the sudden wave of weakness that surged through her almost knocked her off her feet. She moved quickly back to her desk and sat down, staring at him, her mouth dry. 'You...what?' she breathed.

'You've offered me a better deal,' he responded in a tone of cool cynicism. 'I might have to wait another twenty years for Carter to hand over the reins to me.'

Jess felt as if she were being strangled by icy fingers. 'You cold-blooded bastard,' she gasped.

'Then that makes two of us, doesn't it?' he countered equably. 'We should be well matched.'

Agitation took her out of her seat and back to the window. 'There's one thing I ought to make clear,' she uttered in a frosty voice. 'I was only talking about a...a business arrangement. I didn't mean to suggest that we...I mean, it won't be a proper marriage. You'll get a share of the company, but that's...that's all.'

'That seems fair enough.'

'So long as that's understood,' she said firmly, turning back to face him. 'If you so much as lay a finger on me, the deal's off.'

'That's fine by me,' he responded, those grey eyes still mocking. 'You're not really my type—far too prickly an armful. I like my women sweet and soft and feminine.'

'Like Lisa, I suppose?' she snapped before she could bite her tongue.

He appeared to give the matter due consideration. 'Mmm. You could be right,' he conceded. He unfolded himself lazily from his chair. 'Well, I'll leave all the arrangements to you. Just let me know where and when.'

'How soon can you come back to the firm?' she asked tensely.

'As soon as we're married.'

She felt herself blushing. 'Thank you,' she stammered. 'I . . . I'll be in touch.'

'Of course. Well, good evening, Jezebel. I'll look forward to hearing from you.' With those taunting words he was gone, leaving her staring at the closed door, feeling vaguely sick.

What had she done? She must have been mad! How on earth could she have said such a crazy thing? Marry Sam? She leaned back in her deeply upholstered leather executive chair, and closed her eyes. She was going to marry Sam. Her breath escaped in a long, juddering sigh, and a tear seeped from beneath her long dark lashes and began to trace slowly down her cheek. She was going to marry Sam.

'Jessica? Is everything all right?'

She opened her eyes and sat up sharply at the sound of Fiona's voice. 'Yes...oh, yes,' she said quickly. 'Er... Sam's coming back to work for us, Fiona.'

'Really? Oh that's marvellous news!'

'Yes. And that's not all.' She took a deep breath. She was going to have to start telling people, so she might as well rehearse it on Fiona. 'We...we're getting married,' she announced weakly.

'Married? Oh, Jessica, that's wonderful! Oh, you must be so happy!'

'Yes...yes, of course I am.' She forced a thin smile. 'I haven't quite got used to it yet,' she explained shakily.

Fiona smiled in moist-eyed sympathy. 'When is it going to be?' she asked.

'Oh, soon. There's no point in waiting.'

'Of course not.' Fiona giggled. 'And I shouldn't imagine Sam Ryder would be the type of man to stand for a long engagement,' she added archly.

Jess shivered. 'No. Well, it's been rather a long day, Fiona. I think I'll go home now. See you in the morning.'

'Oh, yes.' Fiona sighed romantically. 'I bet you won't sleep a wink tonight!'

'Probably not,' Jess agreed wryly.

That much proved true, at least. Jess lay in her bed, staring up at the shadowy ceiling, her mind a cauldron of emotions. The one thing she tried the hardest not to think about was the one thought that surfaced again and again in her brain. She hadn't really asked Sam to marry her to save the company. She had asked him because she had been torn by jealousy at the thought of his marrying Lisa. And the reason she had been jealous was that she was in love with him.

Well, now she had got him, and the thought gave her no comfort at all. She remembered the casual way he had said, 'I'll leave the arrangements to you—just let me know where and when.' Not for her the joy of loving discussions about whether to have a big reception or just an intimate little gathering for a few friends, whether or not to have a honeymoon. It was purely a business arrangement—agree terms, sign a contract.

But of course it was a lot more complicated than that. Like Fiona, everyone would be expecting her to show signs of being blissfully happy. Fortunately, because she was divorced, it would have to be a register office ceremony. She didn't think she could bear to stand in church and repeat those solemn vows, knowing that Sam didn't mean a word of them.

And then there was afterwards. With a dawning horror she began to realise what it would be like to live with him, day after day, sharing meals, using the same bathroom... How on earth could she do that? Oh, she couldn't go through with it!

But as she hugged the pillow with savage strength, she realised that if she didn't go through with it, he would marry Lisa. It was all or nothing. And she couldn't let him go. With a sob of despair she buried her face in the pillow, and let the bitter tears flow.

CHAPTER FIVE

SHE must have fallen asleep a little before dawn. She woke late, her head aching, wishing she could believe that the events of the previous afternoon had been no more than a bad dream. She took a warm shower, dressed quickly, and set off to drive to work.

Curtains of damp mist hung low over London. The pavements were dark, and people hurried along, huddled into their overcoats, unsmiling and impatient. The north-bound traffic was snarled up by roadworks near Vauxhall Bridge; Jess punched her way aggressively through the jam and swung the Porsche into the southbound lane, raising a storm of protest from half a dozen car horns. She was not in the best of tempers when she arrived at the office.

Fiona was still wearing that romantic smile. 'Oh, good morning, Jessica,' she greeted her brightly. Jess glanced at her sharply. There was an air of secretive delight about her this morning. 'Er...are you going straight into your office?' she enquired.

Jess frowned. 'Of course,' she confirmed, puzzled.

Fiona positively bounced over to the door, and opened it with a flourish. 'Tah-rah!' she cried excitedly.

On Jess's desk was a vase of long-stemmed roses. Twelve of them. Her heart sank into her shoes. 'Was there a card?' she asked weakly.

'They didn't need a card,' declared Fiona. 'Who else would send you red roses? And in November, too. Oh, I never guessed that Sam was so romantic!'

'Nor did I,' murmured Jess drily. 'Well, they can't stay there. They'll be in the way. They'd better go over on the filing cabinet.'

Fiona shot her a hurt look as she moved the vase. 'I wish someone would send me flowers like that,' she grumbled, half to herself.

Jess smiled. 'Oh, I know. They're very nice. Get Sam on the phone for me, would you?'

Fiona retreated to her own office satisfied, and Jess sat down. The roses seemed to glow with their own inner light, and their beautiful perfume filled the air. She drank it in deeply. Just for a moment, she could almost pretend...

The telephone trilled, and she picked it up. Sam's sardonic tone broke the spell. 'Good morning, Jezebel,' he drawled. 'What did you want?'

'Just to thank you for the flowers, Sam,' she said, controlling her voice with difficulty.

'Oh yes, the flowers. Don't mention it. I thought we ought to keep up appearances.'

'Yes. Well, thank you, anyway.' She heard a giggle in the background, and her spine tensed. 'I'm sorry, did I wake you up, Sam?' she enquired sharply.

'No, you didn't wake me,' came the laconic response. 'I've been awake for some time. I just haven't got out of bed yet.'

'I see.' There was that giggle again, followed by some strange noises and then the sound of a playful slap. 'Well, since I gather you're not alone, I won't keep you. There were one or two things I thought we ought to discuss—perhaps at a more convenient time?'

'Sure. What about lunch? Let me see—the day after tomorrow suit you?'

'Thank you. Kind of you to find time to fit me in,' she rapped tartly.

'That's OK. I'll meet you at the George and Dragon, about one o'clock. Got to go now.' The last words were muffled, and the phone went dead with a click.

Jess put the receiver down, her hand trembling with anger and hurt. Who was he with? Lisa? Or did he have other girlfriends besides Lisa? And the worst of it was, she didn't dare let him see that she cared. She was going to have to detach herself from her feelings, lock her aching heart away in some remote corner of her mind and try to forget about it.

Sam was late arriving for their lunch date, and Jess felt herself hating him for that. Even in such liberated times, she felt dreadfully uncomfortable walking into a crowded pub by herself and ordering herself a drink. She received a number of interested glances, until she buried herself defensively behind a copy of the *Financial Times*. She was sure Sam had deliberately suggested that location to cause her embarrassment.

She saw him walk in and go up to the bar, but she kept her attention on the jumbled figures on the page a little longer. Why was it that every time she saw him, her heart began to race like that? It wasn't fair—she didn't seem to have any effect on him.

His grey eyes searched through the crowded room and found her, and he saluted her sardonically. She returned him a thin-lipped smile, and began to fold up her paper as he came towards her, his strong fingers curled round a pint of beer. He had on a well worn leather jacket that seemed to emphasise the powerful width of his shoulders, and Jess felt a sudden weak desire to be held against that hard chest, to feel the warmth of his arms around her.

But she couldn't afford to indulge such thoughts, she scolded herself grimly. She tilted her chin at a proud angle, and said coldly, 'Good afternoon, Sam. I'm glad you could make it. I hope I'm not keeping you from anything important.'

'What could be more important than my own wedding?' he responded in a mocking tone.

Jess took a sip of her Martini to give herself a few seconds to compose herself. 'I've made a list of the things that need to be sorted out,' she said crisply, opening her briefcase and taking out her notepad.

He took it from her, and gave it a cursory glance. 'Date,' he read. 'Well, there's no point in hanging around. Why don't you get a special licence?'

'A special licence?' she repeated weakly.

'Sure. We might as well get it over with. And if you want me to get that Sports Complex business sorted out, the quicker I make a start the better.'

'Don't you have to work out your notice for Bob Carter first?'

'We agreed I shouldn't bother.'

Jess nodded. She had guessed that Bob would be furious at his defection—to say nothing of Lisa's reaction. 'Very well, I'll get a special licence,' she agreed. 'That would mean we could get married on...

Monday.' She hoped he wouldn't notice the tremor of nerves in her voice.

'OK. What's this? Guest-list? I don't have anyone to invite.'

'Oh. Well, nor do I really. So it probably isn't worth bothering with a reception.'

'No. We can scrap the honeymoon idea, too.' He tossed the notepad back to her. 'Anything else?'

Jess felt a rage of disappointment burning inside her. Did he have to treat it all so dismissively? She hesitated a moment, and then said unsteadily, 'There was just one more thing.' He lifted an enquiring eyebrow. 'The question of where we're going to live.'

He shrugged his shoulders to indicate total indifference, far more interested in the huge plate of steak-and-kidney pudding the barmaid had brought him. 'Mmm, thanks, Chrissie,' he said as she set it before him, leaning far closer over his shoulder than was really necessary.

'Just as you like it, Sam,' she giggled. 'Hot and steaming.'

'That's right. You know me well.'

'I like to look after a man with a good appetite,' she pouted, and cast Jess a hostile glare before turning her back and swaying provocatively away. Sam let his eyes follow her across the room before turning back to his lunch with a smile of satisfaction. It was several seconds before he seemed to recall Jess's presence, and he glanced up at her innocently. 'I'm sorry, what were you saying?' he asked politely.

Her jaw was rigid with tension, and she found it difficult to speak. 'Accommodation. We have to decide where we're going to live after...after we're married. I don't really want to give up the lease on my flat.'

'Suits me. I'm virtually squatting at the moment anyway.'

'You'll move into my flat?'

'Well, that seems like the simplest thing to do. I'll fetch my stuff over on Sunday. Any other problems?'

'I don't think so.'

He grinned at her, that taunting gleam in his eyes. 'Don't you want me to sign in blood that I won't attempt to violate your chastity?' he drawled with lazy mockery.

Jess snapped her briefcase shut and stood up. 'I don't think that will be necessary,' she answered in a strained voice.

'You're willing to trust my word of honour?' he taunted.

'Not at all,' she responded. 'I'll simply rely on the fact that you may be assured that if you make any attempt to break that part of the agreement, I shall divorce you at once, and you'll lose everything.'

He laughed softly. 'Oh, you'll be safe enough, Queen Jezebel,' he assured her. 'I told you before, you're not my type.'

'How very fortunate. Well, I'll wish you good afternoon. I'll expect you on Sunday.' She turned him an aloof shoulder, and stalked away.

'Mark, it's three o'clock in the morning.'

'I don't care what the hell time it is.'

'You're drunk.'

'You bet I'm drunk. How the hell do you think I felt when I found out? The least you could have done was tell me yourself.'

'Yes, well...I'm sorry, I was going to, but... Look, we can't stand here arguing about it out here in the corridor. There are other tenants in this block.'

'So let me come inside.'

Jess eyed him warily. 'If I do, do you promise not to make a scene?' she asked. He nodded. 'OK then.' She held the door open for him, and he stepped inside a little unsteadily. 'You look as if you could do with some black coffee,' she suggested drily.

'I could use another drink,' he mumbled.

'Don't you think you've had enough?'

'Not by half.' He threw himself down on to the sofa, and stared at her with slightly unfocused eyes. 'Why did you do it, Jess? What's he got that I haven't?'

'A degree in Civil Engineering,' she offered diffidently.

He scowled. 'Don't give me that. You're not marrying a piece of paper. Oh, I know—he's tall, dark and handsome, and he's swept you off your feet. I suppose I just don't measure up.'

Jess sighed patiently. 'Look, Mark, you know I like you a lot, but I was always honest with you. I was never in love with you.'

'And you're in love with that guy?'

Jess felt her cheeks tinge with pink. 'Well, I am going to marry him,' she defended.

'I'll tell you what,' declared Mark, leaning forward earnestly. 'He's making a fool of you, Jess. He's only after your money.'

Jess laughed. 'I haven't got much money,' she stated grimly. 'It's all tied up in the business, and that isn't doing too well.'

'You know he's still seeing Lisa?'

'They're old friends.'

'They looked a lot more than old friends to me, canoodling on the dance floor at La Belle's.' He rose to his feet and began pacing impatiently round the room.

'If all he wanted was to marry money, he could have married her,' Jess pointed out.

'Maybe Daddy's one step too clever for our Mister Tough-Guy Ryder,' sneered Mark. 'Maybe he won't let his little girl do something she'd regret.'

Jess ran her hand back through her hair with a weary sigh. 'Look, Mark, I just don't want to discuss it with you. It was all over between us already anyway. It would never have worked out.'

He sat down again heavily. 'You never gave it a chance,' he sulked.

'I'm going to make some coffee. I want some, even if you don't,' she said with a thin smile.

'I want the bathroom.'

'Well, you know where it is.'

She went into the kitchen, and filled the kettle. She felt absolutely wrung-out. Mark's unwelcome arrival was just about the last straw. It had been awful, making the arrangements for the wedding on her own. The least Sam could have done was come with her to enter their notice at the register office. It made the whole thing seem so arid and formal, stripped of even the slightest pretence of romance.

Not that his presence was going to make any difference to that, she reflected wryly. It was Saturday night—or rather Sunday morning—and he would be moving in later that day. She had hardly slept a wink all night, thinking about it, trying to imagine what it would be like to have him sleeping in the next room, so near...

The kettle boiled, and she made the coffee—black for Mark—and carried it through to the sitting-room. Mark seemed to be taking an awfully long time over his trip to the bathroom. Cautiously, she went in search of him.

The bathroom was empty. But the door to her bedroom was open, and she could hear the sound of snoring. She peered inside. Mark's clothes were scattered all over the floor, and he was sprawled across the bed, fast asleep. With a helpless shrug, she went over and pulled the quilt up to cover him. Then she went back into the sitting-room, sank into an armchair, and closed her eyes.

The sound of the doorbell jolted her awake, and she stared around in shock. It was daylight, and it took her a moment or two to remember why she had fallen asleep in the armchair. She felt stiff and uncomfortable as she levered herself to her feet. A glance at the clock told her it was only a little after eight. Who could be calling at this hour? Surely not...not Sam already?

But when she opened the door, it was Sam's handsome face that grinned down at her, the eyes mocking as he took an appreciative survey of her slender figure. Blushing self-consciously, she drew the silk of her wrap closer around her body.

'Good morning, beloved,' he greeted her cheerfully, pushing the door wide open with his foot. He was carrying two large canvas holdalls, and there were a couple of cardboard boxes on the floor. 'Well, aren't you going to invite me in?'

She stepped aside, casting an anxious glance at her bedroom door. If Mark should wake up, and come out into the hall . . . Even as the thought crossed her mind, the worst happened. Grumbling, and pushing his tousled fair hair back from his bleary eyes, Mark appeared in the doorway. He was wearing only a pair of underpants, emblazoned in red with the legend 'Superstud.' Jess closed her eyes, and leaned back weakly against the wall. 'Ooops,' she murmured wryly.

'What a masterly understatement,' agreed Sam, his voice rich with cynical amusement. 'Does this sort of thing happen to you often?'

She flashed him a fulminating glare. 'I didn't know you intended to arrive at the crack of dawn,' she accused.

'Oh, yes. I agree it's entirely my fault,' he conceded equably. 'Sorry, old chap,' he added to Mark, mimicking his public-school accent, 'didn't mean to encroach on your time. I wasn't really due until later.'

Mark's face darkened in fury as he heard that mocking voice. He withdrew into the bedroom, slamming the door, and emerged a moment later fully dressed. He marched past them and out of the flat, his head held at a haughty angle.

'Mind the . . .' There was a crash, and a savage oath from the landing. ' . . . boxes,' finished Sam.

Jess hurried to the door. Mark was just picking himself up from the floor. 'Mark! Are you all right?' she gasped anxiously.

'What a damn stupid place to leave them,' glowered Mark in fury. 'I could have broken my neck.' He brushed aside Jess's attempts to help him up. 'I can manage, leave me alone. Ooh, my head.' He staggered into the lift, still sulking as the doors closed on him.

'Sorry if I broke up something interesting,' remarked Sam as he picked up one of the boxes and carried it into the flat.

'You didn't,' Jess grated tersely.

He lifted a quizzical eyebrow. 'No? I have to admit, he did look as if he'd been hitting the bottle a bit too hard to be much use to you,' he commented. 'He was pretty far gone when I saw him earlier in the evening.'

'Oh, yes. He told me he'd seen you. With Lisa.'

'Uh-huh.'

'You don't deny it then?'

He glanced at her in innocent surprise as he went back outside to fetch the other box. 'No . . . why on earth should I?' he asked.

'Oh, no reason,' she rapped tersely. 'This is your room.'

She opened the door for him as he carried the boxes through. He glanced around assessingly. 'Mmm—not bad. Mind if I give it a lick of paint?'

'No—of course not. It's your room,' she agreed with difficulty.

'Fine. I might put up a few shelves—I seem to have collected rather a lot of books again, and there's my hi-fi. You like Charlie Parker?'

'I don't really know much about jazz.'

'I can see I'm going to have to educate you.'

He was smiling, and Jess felt her heart beating a little too fast. 'I...I have to go out this morning. You'd better have a key,' she suggested unsteadily.

'Oh, yes, sure. Thanks.' He took the offered key from her, and threaded it on to a jangling bunch he took from his pocket.

'Er...would you like a cup of coffee or something?' she asked him.

'That'd be nice.' He humped the holdalls through into his room. 'Any chance of some breakfast?'

She couldn't stop herself enquiring sarcastically, 'Didn't Lisa give you any?' The mocking laughter that sprang to his eyes made her instantly regret her slip. She turned him an aloof shoulder, and stalked into the kitchen. He followed her a moment later, and perched himself on one of the stools at the breakfast-bar. 'What do you want to eat?' she asked.

'Oh, not a lot. A couple of fried eggs and a couple of rashers of bacon. And you could fry up some bread and tomatoes while you're at it. Got any sausages?'

'You call that "not a lot"?' she enquired drily.

He grinned self-deprecatingly. 'There's a lot of me to feed,' he pointed out.

'I can see that.' In just a few moments he had taken over her flat, as he had previously taken over her office. And yet she found a strange pleasure in cooking for him, even though his gargantuan fry-up filled her clean kitchen with its aroma. She made two cups of coffee, and sat at the far end of the breakfast-bar, watching him eat.

He cleared the plate with relish. 'That was OK,' he approved. 'This might not prove to be a bad idea after all.'

Jess retreated quickly behind her frosty façade, lest he should suspect the silly dreams that were running through her head. 'Don't get too used to it,' she advised him coolly. 'Cooking and cleaning for you isn't part of the deal. I have a very good housekeeper who comes in during the week. At weekends you can fend for yourself.'

'That's OK,' he agreed without concern. 'I probably won't be at home much anyway.'

'Good. Well, I'd better go and get dressed now. I'll see you later.' She escaped to her own room and closed the door, leaning against it with a sigh. The sight of the tousled bed made her groan. Damn Mark! His presence—not to mention the state he was in—had confirmed to Sam everything that he thought of her.

Well, why should she care, after all? He had been with Lisa last night. Pride lifted her head. The last thing she wanted was for Sam to guess how she felt about him. Let him think the worst of her. Better that he should believe that she had spent last night in a passionate clinch with Mark than that he should guess that she'd spent most of it lying awake indulging the foolish fantasy that their forthcoming marriage was not going to be an empty charade.

It was a relief to have a good excuse to go out. She was to attend a church service and luncheon in Guildford, celebrating the centenary of a local charity that she and Angus had supported. The stately hush of the ceremony, and the cool formality of the gathering, were balm to her spirit. Every move was predictable—a welcome change from Sam's anarchic invasion of her life.

But returning to her flat in the middle of the afternoon she was stunned to find it filled with the smell of paint and curry, and Sam sprawled on her sofa with a can of beer in his hand, watching the rugby on the television. 'Make yourself at home,' she invited tartly.

He glanced up at her with that innocent expression she was learning to mistrust. 'What? Oh, thanks. Help yourself to a beer. There's plenty in the fridge.'

She stalked into the kitchen, trying not to breathe in the pungent aroma of the curry, and tugged open the fridge door. Her cottage cheeses and fresh orange juice had been thoroughly elbowed aside by several cans of beer, a large gammon steak, and a slab of cheddar as thick as a door-post.

'Give that curry a stir, would you?' he called from his recumbent position.

She regarded the saucepan with caution. 'Are you sure it's safe to get that close?' she enquired drily.

But his attention was entirely on the game, throwing up his fist with a whoop of delight as his team evidently scored.

The corners of her mouth drawn into a wry expression, she ventured to investigate his taste in interior design. Pushing open the door of her spare room, she stood on the threshold, staring in astonishment. On her pristine white walls he had painted migraine-inducing zig-zag stripes in solid black.

'What on earth ... ?'

'Do you like it?' he enquired, coming close up behind her. 'It isn't quite finished yet—I've got to put the yellow in.'

'Yellow?'

'Yes—a thin yellow line above the black. It's a good job it's such a big room, otherwise it wouldn't work.'

'No, I don't suppose it would,' she conceded weakly. 'And what's happened to the carpet?'

'I took it up. It's a shame to cover these beautiful floorboards—and you have to agree it wouldn't have gone with the colour-scheme.'

'Oh, I'll agree with that!' she breathed.

'You don't like it,' he perceived at last. His grey eyes were alight with good-humoured mockery, and Jess's lips twitched in reluctant response. He really was impossible!

'I'll just have to keep the door closed, won't I?' she said repressively, and quickly retreated to the sanctuary of her own room.

But his take-over continued unabated. All evening, and far into the night, the music of his jazz records and the sounds of his painting, drilling and hammering disturbed her peace, until her nerves were in shreds.

Morning brought no respite. She was never at her best first thing in the morning, and to walk into her bathroom to find a naked man shaving over her sink really was the last straw. Colour rushed to her cheeks, and she closed her eyes quickly as he turned round. 'Couldn't you have at least locked the door?' she asked weakly.

'I'm sorry. I didn't realise you'd be embarrassed.'
He laughed mockingly. 'I thought you were a woman
of the world.'

'Did you? Well, let me inform you that I'm not
accustomed to...to this sort of thing.'

'No? What about your legions of boyfriends? Don't
they shave?' he taunted.

She opened her eyes in indignation—and closed
them again quickly. 'I'm going to get some breakfast,'
she murmured, beating a hasty retreat.

But at least she couldn't complain of his appearance, she reflected later when they were ready to
set off. He was looking very smart, in an oatmeal-
coloured jacket and slim brown slacks with knife-edge
creases, and his thick dark hair curled crisply around
his handsome head. Most girls would envy her, to be
marrying a man like that—but not if they knew the
truth of the situation.

'We'd better go in my car,' she suggested as he
helped her into her coat.

'We won't,' he countered promptly. 'I don't like
women drivers.'

She stared at him. 'Well, of all the... I'm certainly
not going in that old Land Rover of yours.'

'Why ever not?'

'It's all dented and rusty.'

'It isn't rust, it's primer. And anyway, what difference does it make? Or did you want to ride to your
wedding in a romantic open carriage, drawn by four
white horses?'

'Of course not,' she snapped. 'But I'm not going
in your car, and that's final.'

'Then we'd better drive there separately, hadn't we?' he concluded, a sharp edge behind the sweet reasonableness of his tone.

They were about to leave the flat when Jess suddenly remembered, 'We don't have any witnesses.'

'Ring Fiona,' he suggested. 'Get her to bring Bill French or someone.'

'There isn't much time...'

'Well, do it now then,' he advised, steering her towards the telephone.

'By special licence!' breathed Fiona when Jess had explained to her why her presence was so urgently required. 'Oh, Jessica, how romantic! I told you Sam wasn't the type of man to hang around,' she added with a giggle.

'Can you meet us at the register office in half an hour?'

'We won't be late. Oh, Jessica, I'm so happy for you.'

Jess sighed as she put the phone down. 'You realise my secretary believes this is the romance of the decade?' she remarked drily to Sam.

'Then we'd better not disappoint her, had we—darling?' he responded, a gleam of evil amusement lighting his grey eyes.

CHAPTER SIX

NOTHING could have been further from Jess's romantic imaginings. It was a dismal day, cold and drizzling with rain. Wrapped up in a braided greatcoat, with high boots and a mock-beaver hat, she felt as if she were heading for the Russian front rather than her own wedding. And the analogy was not altogether inapt, she told herself wryly as she parked her red Porsche next to Sam's Land Rover in the car park of the register office.

Fiona rushed forward to greet her, pressing a small bouquet of white roses into her hands. 'What on earth . . . ?' she queried, staring at them.

'We stopped at the florists,' Fiona explained. 'I knew you'd have forgotten the essentials. Bill's brought one of the instant-print cameras from the office, as well.'

'How nice,' murmured Jess weakly.

'Come along then,' urged Sam, taking Jess's hand in a firm grip. 'Let's go in.' Jess felt a shimmer of heat run through her at his touch, but not by a quaver did she let herself betray the aching longing in her heart.

There was something about the very simplicity of the proceedings that touched her deeply—no flowery declarations and promises, just a plain statement that Samuel James Ryder took Jessica Helen Marguerite McGill to be his lawful wedded wife, and vice versa.

As they stepped outside, the sun was shining. The wet pavements gleamed with a million diamonds, and Jess was suddenly struck by how very beautiful London could look on the most unexpected occasions.

'Smile,' urged Bill, raising the camera.

Obediently they smiled and posed for the camera, and gazed with fake adoration into each other's eyes for a second shot.

'There!' beamed Fiona with satisfaction. 'Aren't you going to kiss her, Sam? You're supposed to kiss the bride, you know.'

Jess tried to pull her hand from Sam's, laughing nervously. 'Oh, not here,' she protested.

He smiled like Satan. 'Why not? We've just got married—I'm sure no one would be shocked.'

As he drew her relentlessly into his arms she glared up at him. 'You bastard,' she grated through clenched teeth. 'You're just taking advantage of the situation.'

'Of course,' he murmured in mocking response. 'This is going to be the last chance I get, remember?'

His mouth closed over hers, hard and demanding, crushing apart her lips. She fought to resist him, but the impact of his raw maleness was sending her senses reeling. She felt the aggressive invasion of his tongue, sweeping into the sweet defenceless valley of her mouth—and she didn't even remember surrendering.

He was holding her in a crushing embrace, so that she could scarcely breathe, every inch of her body curved against his with an intimacy that flamed her blood. Her hands reached up to grip his powerful shoulders, moved round to curl in the crisp hair at the nape of his neck. She was letting herself be swept away, forgetting everything but the raging hunger his kiss had ignited inside her.

It was the click of Bill's camera, and Fiona's nervous giggle, that dragged her back to reality. 'Jessica, Sam,' she whispered urgently. 'People are staring.'

Jess drew back, dazed, as Sam let her go. A passing taxi-driver leaned out of his window to yell approvingly, 'That's the way to do it!' and two workmen on the back of a truck were applauding loudly. Her cheeks flamed scarlet, and as Sam dropped his arm around her shoulder she ducked gratefully into its protective shield.

Sam glanced at his watch. 'Well, I think we could have just one drink, to celebrate, don't you?' he suggested.

'Good idea,' agreed Bill without hesitation. 'There's a nice little pub just round the corner from here, and it won't be too crowded yet.'

The pub was welcomingly warm, and they settled themselves at a quiet corner table to look at the photographs Bill had taken.

'I think they've come out really well, considering,' remarked Fiona. 'It was lucky, the sun coming out like that, just at the right moment.' She smiled, dreamy-eyed. 'It must have been an omen.'

'To Sam and Jessica,' toasted Bill. 'May all your troubles be little ones!'

'To Sam and Jessica,' agreed Fiona warmly.

'Well,' joked Bill when the drinks were finished, 'I suppose you and I had better be getting back to work, Fiona, or the boss will be on our tails.' He grinned at Sam, and offered his hand. 'Congratulations, Sam,' he said sincerely. 'And welcome back to the company. We sorely need you.'

'So I gather,' Sam responded drily. 'I'll see you later, Bill. We'll be following you back.'

'You're coming into the office today?' gasped Fiona.

'I'm afraid so,' Sam told her with a rueful smile. 'As Bill so rightly pointed out, things aren't too good at the moment. Our own happiness will have to wait, won't it, darling?'

Jess looked up at him, startled out of her own thoughts. She had been looking at the photographs again. 'Oh...yes. There's plenty of time,' she murmured vaguely.

'The rest of our lives.' He lifted her hand to his lips, and kissed it lightly, but the eyes that held hers gleamed with mockery.

No one even bothered to pretend that she was still the boss of McGill Construction. She still had her spacious office, with its desk and telephone, she still had her secretary, but she had nothing to do. 'Fiona, where's the Abbeycourt Estate file?' she asked, walking into the outer office.

'I've got it,' Sam told her, glancing up from Fiona's desk, where he was signing letters.

'Where's Fiona?'

'She's in my office, sorting through a bunch of old contracts for me.'

'Oh. She seems to work for you more than she does for me these days,' Jess commented tartly.

He didn't even seem to notice her irritation. 'She's very useful to me,' he answered, continuing with what he had been doing. 'She knows the business inside out.'

'And what am I supposed to do while she's working for you?'

He looked up at her again. 'What did you want her for?'

'To find the Abbeycourt file.'

'I just told you—I've got it.'

Jess ground her teeth, struggling against her rising anger. 'I thought I'd check on our progress there.'

He finished signing the letters, and closed the blotting-book. 'We're doing very well. I was going to have a word with you about it.'

'Oh?' That one word was rich with sarcastic amazement that he was actually going to discuss any facet of the business with her.

'I think it would be worth setting up a couple of show-homes on the site. I thought you could take it on—if you're not too busy, of course.'

'Oh, no.' Her voice shook with ironic laughter. 'Of course I'm not too busy. In fact I don't have a thing to do—you're doing it all.'

His eyes flickered with amusement. 'I thought that was the general idea.'

'Oh . . . I suppose so.' She felt cross with herself because she knew she was being unreasonable. 'But I didn't mean you to take over and leave me nothing to do.'

He laughed. 'Look, I was serious about the show-homes. And there's quite a few other projects where it would be useful to have some design input ourselves, in addition to the technical aspects.'

Jess's fist was clenching and unclenching in agitation. She was sure he was just fobbing her off with something to do to keep her quiet, and yet... 'All right,' she conceded. 'But I'll need the file. I'll have to have a look at the layouts and the sizes of the rooms.'

'I'll send it over.'

But if Jess found it frustrating to stand aside and let Sam run everything his way, she had to admit that he knew what he was doing. He had set about reorganising every division, offering some of the staff redundancy payments, but there wasn't a shred of resentment. Everyone agreed it was just the shot in the arm the firm needed. And already two worthwhile contracts had been signed.

The office Christmas party was held in a spirit of optimism that Jess had feared would never return to the company. The accounts office were hosting it this year. All the computers had been switched off and pushed back against the walls to leave a big open space in the middle of the room, and festoons of paperchains had been strung across the ceiling.

An 'entertainment' had been arranged. This was an old McGill custom. Each year, the departments hosting the party vied with each other to produce the silliest pantomime, full of broad caricatures of senior members of staff and a variety of in-house jokes. As the supermarket wine and canned lager flowed, Jess glanced around the laughing, happy faces, and felt a small glow of satisfaction. McGill Construction was going to survive. Was any sacrifice too great to achieve that?

Her eyes sought around the crowded room to find Sam. He was leaning against one of the filing cabinets, chuckling with amusement as the brawniest of the accountants, dressed in a pink net tutu that was far too tight for him, camped around the 'stage' sprinkling fairy-dust over everyone in range.

She had never seen him laugh like that, without mockery, and her heart contracted suddenly. If only things could have been different between them. Oh, he was civil enough to her, when he was at home—which was rarely. He kept most of the time to his own room, playing his music and reading his books, unless there was a rugby match or a good film on the television. He certainly showed not the least inclination to break the terms of their contract.

But at Christmas, with all the warmth that flowed, even between strangers, maybe that icy barrier between them could melt a little. But she would have to make the first move. Taking a deep, steadying breath, she stood up. But at that moment the pretty little blonde from reception approached him, engaging his attention with her fluttery false eyelashes and her sweet 'Strawberry Sunrise' smile.

Jess hesitated, and turned away to speak to someone else. She would try again later, when the girl had moved on. But the girl didn't move on; she stayed beside him, sharing more jokes than the ones in the pantomime. And when the show finished to a welter of cheers and someone put on some music for people to dance to, he seemed to need little persuasion to lead her out on to the floor.

Jess circulated, chatting to everyone, patiently waiting for her opportunity to approach Sam. The lights had been turned low, and the Christmas spirit, much of it blended and bottled in Scotland, was ripening several casual friendships. Sam was holding the girl far too close, and did he have to smile down into her eyes in quite that intimate way?

The party wore on. Jess danced with Bill French, and with Carl from the Roads Division, and with the chief accountant, and all the while Sam stayed with the blonde. People had started to notice, and there was a good deal of whispering and giggling going on about it. She tried hard to pretend it didn't matter, but her smile was brittle and there were tears stinging the back of her eyes.

And then suddenly he was gone, and so was the blonde. The realisation struck her like a body-blow. 'Jessica, are you all right?'

She glanced round into Fiona's anxious face. 'Oh— yes. It's just a little warm in here,' she answered quickly.

Fiona nodded, a sympathy in her eyes that made Jess want to scream. 'You've had a row with Sam, haven't you?' she asked gently.

'What? Oh . . . yes, it was a silly thing really, something and nothing.' She laughed weakly.

'I thought so. Don't worry about it, Jessica. He'll come round—they always do. My Ron goes off in a huff every now and then, but it blows over.'

'Yes . . . thank you. I think I'll go outside for a little while—get some fresh air.'

'Of course.'

She *wasn't* looking for him. She was just . . . glancing into all the empty offices to see that everything was all right. She couldn't help noticing that his coat had gone. Yes, dammit, she *was* looking for him. She couldn't hold back the tears as she hurried down the stairs, and across the road to the car park.

The Land Rover wasn't where he had parked it this morning. Of course, he might have moved it, though she didn't remember him going out. She walked back slowly down the echoing stairwell. This was where she had first met him. She touched the wall where they had stood, as if a time-warp could spin her back to that moment, and she could start over again, wiser.

But there could be no going back. She took a deep breath, composing herself with an effort of will. She wasn't going to make a fool of herself—especially in front of her own staff.

The party was breaking up when she got back. The lights were on, revealing a blitzed debris of empty paper cups and half-eaten sandwiches. Some of the secretaries had started to clear up, and Jess joined in to help. 'Oh, you needn't do this, Jessica,' Fiona protested as soon as she noticed. 'It won't take us long. Why don't you get along home? You look worn out.'

'Perhaps I will. Thank you,' Jess agreed gratefully. 'Well, goodbye then, Fiona. Have a nice Christmas.'

'I will. And the same to you.'

'Thank you.' She went to fetch her coat, exchanging cheerful good wishes with several of her staff, and then walked back across to the car park where she had left her Porsche. She sank back into the deep leather bucket-seat, and closed her eyes. She didn't want to go home yet—she knew Sam wouldn't be there. Usually she could pretend to herself when he was away that he was working. She never questioned him. But this evening was different—this evening she knew where he was. And she could visualise every move so clearly in her mind.

No! She mustn't do this to herself. She shook her head to clear it, and turned the ignition key. The engine roared into life, and she spun the wheel as she reversed neatly out of her parking space. She wanted to drive fast, let the car have its head. Without even thinking about where she was going, she turned towards the Old Kent Road.

She squeezed through the traffic around the one-way system at New Cross, past the shabby neglected tenements by Deptford Bridge, and then she was soaring across Blackheath, and away along the long straight stretch of Shooters Hill. The night was dark enough for highwaymen; the windscreen-wipers beat a steady, comforting rhythm as she put her foot down and raced out into the emptiness of Kent.

It was almost ten o'clock when she got home. She knew as soon as she opened the door that the flat was empty. She took her coat off, and went straight into the kitchen to prepare herself a light snack before going to bed.

Tomorrow was Christmas Eve. She had made lots of plans for a real traditional Christmas, even though there would be only the two of them. She would try to forget about what had happened this afternoon—after all, she couldn't really blame him for seeking his entertainment elsewhere, under the circumstances. Tomorrow she would really try to put things right.

Sam didn't come home all night. Jess spent a happy morning in the kitchen, baking mince pies and making the stuffing and the brandy butter to go with their

Christmas dinner. She was a little surprised when she looked at the time. Where had he got to? She laid the pies out carefully on a wire tray to cool, and went out to get a few last-minute bits of shopping.

When she got back, the flat was still empty, but Sam's door was ajar, and the clothes he had been wearing yesterday were on the bed. And one of the mince pies was missing from the kitchen, leaving only a few flakes of pastry to show where it had been stolen. She smiled to herself. He'd probably just popped out for some late shopping too. He'd be home soon.

But he didn't come home—not all that night, nor all the next day. She wavered between tears and anger. His present waited for him beneath the tinsel-decked Christmas tree—it was the new novel by one of his favourite authors, and she had taken so much pleasure in choosing it and wrapping it in bright gift-paper.

At some moments she imagined him coming home, expecting to be met by a scold, and she would give him his present with a special little smile ... At others she made up her mind to take it away, and return it to the shop after Christmas.

Occasionally she wondered if she ought to check with the police—after all, he might have had an accident—but she couldn't bring herself to admit to some anonymous young constable that her husband of just a few weeks had gone off with a pretty blonde at the office Christmas party.

He finally came home the day after Boxing Day. He strolled in as if nothing had happened, and it took all Jess's self-control to remain calm. 'Hi,' he greeted her cheerfully. 'Did you have a nice Christmas?'

'Yes, thank you,' she responded coolly. 'I did wonder where you'd got to.'

'I went to stay with friends,' he explained with no trace of concern. 'I assumed you'd made arrangements of your own.'

Pride came to her rescue. 'Of course. I just wished you'd mentioned that you wouldn't be home at all.'

'Didn't you see my note?' He glanced over at the sideboard. 'Oh, it's fallen over. No wonder you didn't see it. Sorry.' He handed it to her, and she glanced at it briefly. *See you after Christmas—enjoy yourself, Sam,* he had scrawled, and a P.S.—*Mince pies smashing—save some for me.* 'Oh, and here's your Christmas present. I didn't have a chance to give it to you.'

He handed her a small box, wrapped in silver paper with a bow on top—shop-wrapped. When she opened it, it was a bottle of her favourite perfume. 'Thank you,' she murmured. 'It's the one I always wear.'

'I know. I recognized it,' he remarked, strolling into the kitchen. 'Any mince pies left?'

'Yes. And I saved you a piece of Christmas cake— I made that myself, too.' She had thrown most of the food away, untouched, not wanting him to guess at the dismal time she had spent waiting for him. 'Oh, and your present's under the tree.'

'Smashing. Just like when I was a kid!' He came out of the kitchen, munching a mince pie, and picked up his present. 'A book! Ah, I was going to get that one—how did you guess?'

Her cheeks tinged with pink with pleasure. 'I thought ... I knew you liked his books.'

'Clever girl.' He leaned over and pecked her lightly on the cheek. 'By the way, Lisa's having a party on New Year's Eve. If you're not doing anything else, why don't you come along?'

Jess froze. 'That sounds nice,' she said, her voice taut. 'I haven't seen Lisa for a few weeks.'

'She's been away.'

'Oh?'

'She went to Mustique with some pop star she's been seeing.'

It was fortunate that he was still leafing with interest through his book, and didn't notice the nuances of expression crossing Jess's face. She took a deep, steadying breath, struggling to regain her composure. 'Lucky thing,' she remarked lightly. 'I bet she's got a fabulous tan.'

'What?' He glanced up. 'Oh yes, she has. I'll tell her you're coming to the party then?'

'Yes.' She hesitated. 'You'll be seeing her then— before the party?'

'I expect so.'

'What about her pop star?'

'Oh, he's gone off on tour.' He closed the book, apparently oblivious to the chaos he had created in Jess's mind. 'Do you want the bathroom for a while? I think I'll take a shower.'

'No... Go ahead,' she managed to say. 'Are you going to be in for lunch? I thought I'd fix something, as Mrs Bird won't be coming in. It'll only be leftovers, I'm afraid.'

'That's fine—thanks,' he said over his shoulder as he strolled off to his own room.

A thousand questions were racing around in Jess's mind as she prepared their snack. If Lisa had been away, where had Sam been on the nights he hadn't come home? With someone else? Or had she misjudged him? Maybe there was still a chance... And yet he was planning to see Lisa before the end of the week—and her boyfriend was away...

She shook her head impatiently. The simplest thing would be to ask him outright if he was still having an affair with Lisa. After all, even though they didn't have a normal marriage, she had a right to know if he was seeing someone else. People would talk...

But she was afraid to do that—afraid that he would guess how important it really was to her. And she wasn't sure that he would tell her the truth, anyway. It would be best to wait until New Year's Eve. She would see them together at Lisa's party. Then she could judge for herself.

She gave a great deal of thought to the subject of what she should wear for the party. She wanted to look stunning, but elegant—and that meant black. In the end she decided to buy a new dress. It was fun to stroll around the shops when they were so quiet. She tried on lots of dresses, but settled at last for one by her favourite designer.

It was a sheath of black silk jersey. The neckline was high, finished with a collar that fitted in soft folds around her throat, and the long, tight sleeves buttoned demurely to the wrist with a dozen tiny buttons. It cost rather more than she had intended to pay, but when she saw her reflection in the mirror she knew that it was worth every penny—the way it clung and moved as she walked had a kind of sensuous grace that was almost feline.

The look in Sam's eyes when she emerged from her room confirmed her instinct. Her only jewellery was a slim gold Belcher chain, and she had put her hair up into a loose bun high on her head, leaving wispy tendrils curling round her face to soften the effect. Her make-up was a work of art, defining her features with a delicate touch of sophistication.

'Ver-ry nice,' Sam approved, letting his gaze drift slowly down over the slender curves of her body.

'Thank you,' she responded with a smile that reflected the lift in her heart. He had been attracted to her once—strongly attracted, if she judged with any accuracy. Maybe...just maybe...if she could get that feeling back...

Sam had chosen to dress formally too, in a black dinner-jacket and black bow-tie; but somehow the very elegance of his clothes underlined the raw maleness that was never disguised by the veneer of urbanity he could adopt when it suited him.

Into Jess's mind, with bewildering clarity, flashed the image of him she had seen in the bathroom on the morning of their wedding: sun-bronzed skin and work-hardened muscles, and a dark scattering of hair across his chest and running down in a line... Her mouth was dry as she turned to let him wrap her rich velvet opera-cloak around her shoulders.

The end of December had brought several heavy falls of snow, and it was piled in dirty heaps along the pavement. Sam hailed a taxi, and as it pulled in to the kerb he scooped Jess up in his arms before she had realised what he was going to do, and carried her through the slush to set her down safely in the back of the cab.

She was laughing breathlessly as he climbed in beside her. 'What did you do that for?'

'A chivalrous impulse. You don't want to get your feet wet tramping through the puddles.'

'No...thank you,' she agreed, her eyes shining as the blood coursed through her veins. It was dark in the back of the cab, and he was so close—she could just reach out her hand and touch him. Instead she brushed a strand of hair back over her shoulder, aware of a tingling electricity in her fingertips as her mind sent conflicting messages.

How could you flirt with your own husband? How could you start that delicious 'getting to know you' game, when you already had his ring on your finger—especially when you'd had to go out on your own and buy that ring yourself? Jess sat gazing blankly out of the window, at a loss to know how to make the next move.

The taxi circled around Sloane Square and turned into the elegant streets of Belgravia, and drew up outside the Carters' discreetly smart town-house. Here the snow had been properly cleared and taken away, and Sam offered Jess his hand to alight from the cab.

The front door was flung open as they walked up the wide, shallow steps. Jess wasn't sure what she had expected of Lisa, but the reality came as a surprise. First, there was her appearance. Her fine, silky hair had been permed into an electric shock of curls that shone around her head like candy-floss. She was very slim and very tanned, and seemed to have been poured into a skimpy dress of shocking pink ruched satin. The effect was sensational.

'Jez!' She extended both hands in a warm gesture of welcome. 'Thank you for coming.' Jess took her hands, and they kissed each other on the cheek as they usually did. 'I'm so glad we can still be friends,' Lisa murmured softly in her ear.

'Of course.' But Jess felt suddenly uncertain again. Lisa had spoken as if she had been expecting her to be angry—but surely it should be the other way round? Lisa was the one who had been jilted...wasn't she? Unless Sam's marriage made no difference to their relationship. Maybe the trip to Mustique, and the pop-star boyfriend, been just a blind to confuse the gossips?

'Isn't it grand?' Lisa was rushing on. 'Mummie and Daddy have gone away for a whole month, and left me with the run of the house. Do come upstairs and take your coat off. I know it's simply freezing outside, but you won't be cold in here, I promise you.'

She bounced up the stairs, her body swaying provocatively in the tight pink satin. Jess didn't glance at Sam to see if he was enjoying the view—she knew that he wouldn't stint himself. She followed more slowly, her mind in turmoil.

'You've got a lovely tan,' she commented as she followed Lisa into one of the magnificent bedrooms. 'When did you get back from Mustique?'

'Just before Christmas. Jimmy had to go straight on to the States to join his band.'

'What a pity. So you just had a family Christmas then?'

'Oh, no. Mummie and Daddy had already left for Monte Carlo.'

Jess didn't dare probe any further. Lisa did not have the look of one who had spent a lonely Christmas.

'What did you do?' Lisa asked, her blue eyes bright and innocent.

Jess turned to the mirror to check her hair. 'Oh, I had a nice, quiet time,' she said cautiously.

'All by yourself?'

You knew Sam wasn't with me! 'Oh, no...of course not,' she lied, controlling her voice with difficulty. 'I was kept quite busy—there were so many people to visit. There—I'm ready. Shall we go down?'

CHAPTER SEVEN

SAM seemed to be very much at home in Lisa's house, with Lisa's friends. As the two girls walked into the imposing drawing-room he was laughing with her cousin—that deep, mellow laugh that Jess liked so much. The two men turned at their approach, and Paul Carter's handsome face creased into a wide smile.

He had always been one of Jess's admirers and she felt reassured by the warm approval in his eyes. Her husband might be having an affair with one of her best friends, but at least she could let him see that she could play the same game if she chose. She deliberately injected an extra degree of warmth into her greeting. 'Paul! How are you?'

He came towards her at once, taking both her hands in his. 'Heartbroken,' he declared theatrically. 'How could you let this oaf sweep you off your feet like that?'

She laughed huskily, flirting with him as she never could with Sam. 'Don't try telling me *your* heart's broken, Paul,' she countered. 'It's on elastic.'

'Unfeeling hussy. Well, I shall just have to make do with a dance. You don't mind if I borrow your wife, do you, Sam?'

'Feel free,' Sam responded laconically. He was talking quietly to Lisa, and Jess's spine was a column of ice as she turned away from him. She wasn't going to let either of them see that she cared.

The furniture in the music-room had been pushed back against the wall, and the carpet rolled up. Several couples were dancing, and Paul drew her into his arms. 'So is it going to be third time lucky then?' he teased.

She smiled, but her eyes evaded his. 'Oh...who knows?' she answered with a casual shrug. 'Maybe I should adopt the motto, "If I survive, I shall have five".'

He laughed, hugging her waist and spinning her round as they danced. 'That's the idea,' he approved. 'No one as gorgeous as you should ever be one man's exclusive property. Let the rest of us poor saps get a look-in too.'

Jess's eyes flashed. 'I certainly wouldn't regard myself as *any* man's exclusive property,' she snapped.

Paul put on a contrite face. 'Oh dear—now I've offended your feminist principles,' he sighed.

'Don't be silly.' Sam had walked into the room with Lisa, and now they were dancing just a few feet away. She made herself smile at Paul. 'It's a party. Let's not discuss anything serious. Why don't we go and get a drink?'

'Whatever you say,' he grinned. 'You must try the punch. Lizzy smuggled back half a dozen bottles of Jamaican rum from her dirty jaunt with the Randy Roadie, and most of it's gone into the punch.'

'Roadie?' queried Jess, interested. 'I thought he was a pop star?'

Paul chuckled. 'No. Who told you that? He calls himself their "Logistics Co-ordinator", but all he does is hump amplifiers.'

Jess's mouth curved into a secret smile. Lisa could never resist those little white lies to 'gild the lily'—

she had been exactly the same at school. Maybe...maybe that was what she was doing with her hints about her relationship with Sam—gilding the lily, making Jess believe something was going on when there wasn't.

She glanced back uncertainly over her shoulder. The pair of them were still dancing very close. Would they be acting like that if they had something to hide? Oh, dammit, she didn't know what to think any more! But as the evening wore on, and Sam stayed at Lisa's side, it was like the Christmas party all over again— except that Lisa was a far more formidable rival than the empty-headed little blonde from the office. So she stayed with Paul, flirting wildly with him in the faint hope that Sam might show a hint of jealousy. But he didn't even seem to notice.

It was a lively party. Jess wondered privately what Miriam Carter would say if she could see the way her daughter had filled her elegant house with noisy revellers, steadily getting drunker as the minutes ticked away towards midnight. For this the punch was largely responsible. Jess had tried a few cautious sips; the fruity taste was deceptively mild, but the potent spirit with which it was laced gave it a kick like a mule—it was dynamite.

'Hey, hush everyone. Three minutes to go. Turn on the radio!' someone was calling.

There was a scramble of excitement. The music stopped, and instead the effervescent tones of a famous disc jockey filled the room. '...really a *lot* of fun going on down here at Trafalgar Square, even without the fountains. And I think...yes, it's time to go over to our Mike, hanging up there by his fingernails from the big clock. Hi there, Mike. What's the situation?'

'Well, I'm just putting my ear-muffs on now, Neville. And it looks to me like the little hand's on twelve, and the big hand's on...yes, it's TWELVE!!!'

Everyone at the party had crossed and linked hands, in an endless twisted chain that wound from room to room. As the chimes rang out, they began to count, 'One, two, three...' As they reached twelve, they broke into a loud chorus of 'Auld Lang Syne', repeated faster and faster until they all broke up in breathless laughter.

'Happy New Year,' smiled Paul, drawing Jess into his arms. She tilted up her face, and let him kiss her. He kissed with expert technique, but all the time she was wondering where Sam and Lisa were, trying to remember when she had last seen them.

'Happy New Year, Paul,' she returned softly, and then the crowd drew them apart as other friends crowded in to exchange kisses. Jess extricated herself from the mêlée as soon as she could, and slipped out into the quiet hallway.

It was a lofty hall, with a marble floor and an imposing brass chandelier hanging low from the ceiling. Jess glanced up the stairs. Had Sam and Lisa slipped away up there? As her footsteps hesitated momentarily, she noticed suddenly that the narrow door leading down to Lisa's flat in the basement was ajar.

Hardly daring to breathe, she pushed the door further open, and listened. She could hear something—a muffled giggle—coming from down there. With infinite caution she stepped inside, and drew the door shut behind her.

There was a strappy pink sandal on the stairs—one that Lisa had been wearing. At the bottom was its twin. She crept down the stairs, and peered round the corner. The sitting-room door was open, and she could see two people on the sofa. They hadn't noticed her, so wrapped up were they in each other's arms. She didn't need to look twice. That dark, ruffled head, and the wide shoulders in the crisp white shirt, were all too painfully familiar.

She drew back hastily, and leaned against the wall, fighting for breath. So it was true! Knowing only that she had to get away, she stumbled up the stairs to the hall. A conga-line was dancing through the house, and before she knew what was happening, she was caught up in it, and heard Paul laughing in her ear. 'There you are, Jess. I was wondering where you'd got to.'

It was easier to join the line than to resist. Blindly she gripped the person in front of her as Paul wrapped his arms around her from behind, and let herself be swept along from room to room. Her mind was numb, replaying over and over again the scene she had witnessed down in the basement flat.

'I need a drink, Paul,' she pleaded as the dancers finally collapsed, exhausted.

'Sure. Want to try some more of that punch?'

'Yes,' she agreed recklessly. 'What the hell? It's New Year. I feel like getting drunk!'

She felt as if she were watching the revelry through a mirror. Streamers and balloons were being tossed about, people were wearing silly hats, blowing on toy trumpets, and performing crazy dances to the kitsch music blasting out of the hired sound-system.

Paul returned with her drink, and she drank it down in a long draught, and handed the glass back to him. 'Boy, I needed that. Any chance of another one?'

He stared at her in astonishment. 'You really *are* going to get drunk,' he breathed. 'I've never seen you drink like that before.'

'Well, maybe it's time I found out what I'm missing,' she suggested carelessly.

She tossed the second drink back as quickly as the first. The rum had warmed her veins, melting the mirror to a strange, distorting mist. Suddenly all the colours in the room seemed brighter, the music louder. She heard herself laughing as someone caught her hand and drew her into the dancing.

Nothing mattered any more. Time was passing erratically, as in a dream. The room was reeling—or was it she that was reeling in a wild hokey-cokey? Paul's arm was tight around her waist, and she laughed up at him as she tripped over her own feet.

'Did you have to get my wife in this state?'

'Maybe you should have looked after her yourself, if you're that bothered.'

'I thought *you* were looking after her.'

'I'd be glad to.'

Jess stared up in bewilderment at the two men who seemed to be arguing above her head.

'I know what your idea of looking after her would mean,' Sam was muttering fiercely.

'Well, what's sauce for the goose is sauce for the gander,' Paul retaliated.

'Mind your own damn business. Jess, sit there while I go and get your coat. And don't move, for heaven's sake.'

'I want another drink,' she protested petulantly.

'Well, you're not having one. You've had more than enough already.'

'Jez? Are you all right?'

The voice of sweet concern was Lisa's, and Jess's teeth clenched in anger. 'Oh, I'm absolutely marvellous, thank you,' she spat venomously.

'You're not going to be sick?'

'No I'm not,' she insisted, hating her for sowing the thought in her mind.

'Come on, try and stand up,' she heard Sam's voice say.

'I told you I'm all right. I just want to go home.' Tears were scalding the backs of her eyes.

'That's exactly where we're going. Donald and Sara are giving us a lift.'

'Good old Donald and Sara!'

'Jess, shut up and put your coat on.' He was beginning to sound really angry.

Somehow she managed to walk to the front door, clumsily wrapping the cloak around her shoulders, but at the first breath of fresh air everything slipped away from her, and she would have fallen if Sam and Lisa hadn't been holding her up. They walked her step by step to the waiting car.

'Goodnight, Lisa. I'm sorry about this,' Sam murmured.

'That's OK,' came the generous response. 'I hope she feels better in the morning.'

'She'll feel terrible in the morning.' He climbed in beside her, and slipped his arm around her shoulders. 'Right, Don,' he said as he shut the car door.

Jess sat in seething silence. There were so many things she wanted to say, but she couldn't say any of them in front of the couple in the front seats. It was warm in the car, and she began to feel sleepy. Her head dropped on to Sam's shoulder, and she gave a soft little sigh of contentment.

She woke with a start as they pulled up outside her block of flats. Sam was thanking Don as he coaxed her carefully out of the car. She swayed unsteadily on her feet, and he cursed under his breath. 'I suppose I'm going to have to carry you.'

Again she was swept up in those strong arms. She seemed to weigh nothing at all as he strode up the steps with her, past the sympathetic night-porter and into the lift. She wrapped her arms around his neck, and tried to smile up at him.

'Are you cross with me, Sam?' she enquired apprehensively.

'Not at all,' was the cool response. 'You're a grown woman—if you want to get drunk and make a fool of yourself, that's entirely up to you. You'll be the one with the bad head in the morning.' He stepped out of the lift, and propped her up against the wall as he opened the door of the flat.

'I didn't make a fool of myself,' she grumbled as he picked her up again. 'Nearly everyone was drunk.'

'Everyone wasn't draped around Paul Carter. Another moment and he'd have been taking you off upstairs to see his etchings.'

She giggled, nestling into his shoulder. 'I wouldn't have gone,' she whispered.

'You didn't look as if you were in a fit state to make that sort of decision,' he remarked derisively, carrying her into her bedroom and dumping her unceremoniously on the bed.

She caught the edge of his jacket as he moved away. 'I wouldn't have gone to bed with Paul,' she insisted, tugging at his jacket.

He laughed as she pulled him down on to the bed, leaning his arm across her to stop himself overbalancing. 'How much have you had to drink?' he asked her.

'Only a couple of glasses of punch.'

'No wonder! That stuff was lethal.'

'It was nice. It's just that I don't usually drink very much.' She cast him a careful look from beneath her lashes, and let her hand slide slowly up his arm until it reached his shoulder. The strength of his powerful muscles beneath the smooth worsted of his jacket thrilled her. She put up her other hand, and linked her fingers around the back of his neck. 'Why don't you invite me up to see *your* etchings?' she suggested huskily.

His mouth curved into a smile of slightly mocking amusement. 'You *are* drunk!' he commented.

She drew herself up towards him. 'Not too drunk to look at etchings,' she murmured.

A breathless tension crackled in the air between them. Jess could hardly believe that she was behaving so wantonly; she would never have dreamt she could have had the courage to seduce anyone—least of all Sam. But the alcohol in her veins had drowned all her inhibitions, and with a small sigh she brushed her lips against his.

For a moment he was as unresponsive as a block of wood, but then his arms were around her, and their mouths melted together in a kiss that seemed to plumb the very depths of her soul. Dizzily she clung to him, barely sensing that he had laid her back on the bed, and was beside her, his hand caressing her body with long, sensuous strokes.

She moved against him invitingly, her spine curving to offer him the aching swell of her breasts. It was almost a relief as he drew down the zip of her dress, and slid the fabric off from one creamy shoulder, but the tension mounted inside her again as his hot mouth began to trace with tantalising slowness down over the delicate shell of her ear and the slender column of her throat.

His hand moved to lift her breast to his mouth as if it were a ripe peach. A quivering shock ran through her as his lips brushed the tender nipple, and she felt the languorous swirl of his tongue, savouring the sweetness of her flesh. She let her head fall back on to the pillow as the giddying race of her blood swept her into a land of fiery whirlpools.

And then his hand moved on, down over the smooth length of her thigh, to slowly draw up the hem of her skirt. She felt his touch glide on the sheer silk of her tights as he coaxed her into surrendering to the most intimate caresses.

He lifted his head and looked down at her. 'Do you want me to go on?'

She gazed up at him through misted eyes. 'Yes,' she whispered pleadingly.

But suddenly he laughed—a harsh laugh that lacerated her unguarded heart. 'Yes. And then tomorrow, when you'd sobered up, you'd be yelling that I took advantage of you, and broke our deal. Well, thanks, but no thanks. No man likes to think he's got to get a woman drunk to make love to her—least of all when that woman happens to be his wife.'

'Sam . . . !'

But he had broken away from her, and was out of reach. His eyes surveyed her coldly. 'You look a mess,' he sneered.

With a sickening wave of humiliation she became aware of how dishevelled she was by his caresses. And suddenly she remembered the way she had seen him with Lisa in his arms. 'Get out of here,' she shouted, trying to sit up and pull her dress straight. 'I hate you. I wouldn't want you to make love to me if I was unconscious.'

His cruel laughter mocked her. 'You very nearly are,' he drawled insultingly, and then he was gone, leaving her alone with her tears of anger and shame.

Sam wasn't there when she woke up the next day. She was rather glad—after his humiliating rejection she needed time to compose herself. She didn't want to let him see any more chinks in her armour. When he didn't come home for several days, she knew he must be with Lisa.

So she was startled to walk into the kitchen on Sunday morning to find him sitting at the breakfast bar, drinking coffee and doing the *Sunday Times* crossword. She was still wearing her nightdress and a thin wrap of silk and lace, but she wasn't going to highlight any sexual tension between them by scuttling off to change. She walked breezily over to the fridge to pour herself a glass of orange juice.

'Good morning,' she remarked, unable to keep the sarcastic edge from her voice. 'It *is* a surprise to see you here. What's happened? Have you and Lisa had a lover's tiff?'

'She's gone skiing,' he answered without concern.

'And you didn't want to go with her?'

'No.'

A demon seemed to be prompting Jess this morning. 'Aren't you afraid she might fall for some handsome ski instructor?' she goaded.

'She's a free agent,' he responded indifferently. ' "I hesitate and stop to counterstroke" '

Jess tipped her head on one side to consider the clue. 'Hesitate...that's usually e-r. So it's i-e-r and stop. Riposte—that means counterstroke, doesn't it?'

'That's right,' he agreed. 'And it fits. Good—I couldn't finish last week's—one of the clues was a real bitch. I thought I was losing my touch.'

'Surely not,' she murmured in mild mockery.

'Is that all you're having for breakfast?' he enquired, glancing at her plate.

'Of course. I'm not a big eater.'

'No wonder you're so skinny,' he teased.

'Oh, I know I'm not *your* type,' she countered haughtily. 'But I regard that as an advantage.'

He surveyed her slender shape appraisingly. 'Do you know, I think you've got even thinner since I've known you,' he remarked. 'You want to be careful—you'll waste away.'

'I'm not wasting away,' she snapped, her nerves tautened by the way he was looking at her.

'Yes, you are. If you went out in a high wind, you'd get blown away.' He smiled that unbelievably attractive smile. 'I'd better take you out to dinner and feed you up.'

Jess felt her heart starting to beat faster. She would love to go out to dinner with him—which was a very good reason not to go. 'I see,' she bit out between clenched teeth. 'While Lisa's away, I can take her place, is that it? Well, no, thank you—I don't play second best to anyone.'

He lifted one eyebrow in quizzical amusement. 'What's wrong?' he taunted. 'You and I don't have the normal sort of husband-and-wife relationship, but at least we can try to be friendly.'

'Friendly?' she retorted in growing agitation. 'It wasn't very friendly of you to make me look a fool in front of everyone at Lisa's party, dancing with her all night. What do you think people are saying behind my back?'

His hard mouth curved into a smile of mocking cynicism. 'This arrangement was your idea,' he reminded her drily. 'You should have given more thought to the small print.'

'I didn't think it would be necessary to ask that you behave with a little discretion,' she threw back at him.

'Oh? Like you, I suppose? Getting so drunk you could hardly stand up?'

'Oh, yes,' she countered, her heart racing so fast that she was short of breath. 'And what were you doing while I was getting drunk? Downstairs in Lisa's flat?'

The smile had curled into a sneer. 'Spying, were you? Well, I was only doing what you'd have been doing with her cousin if I hadn't intervened,' he snapped back. 'And probably have done on numerous occasions of which I'm unaware.'

'Oh, no,' she declared with dignity. 'You can't accuse me of that. I've never had an affair—not before our marriage or since.'

He stared at her in open disbelief. 'You've never had an affair? Who are you trying to kid? I wasn't born yesterday.'

'It's true,' she insisted, wishing she hadn't blurted out her secret but now determined to convince him. 'I've never slept with anyone in my life.'

'Oh, come on!' he sneered. 'You've got two ex-husbands, for a start.'

'I know, but . . . I never slept with either of them. I left the first the day we got married, and the second . . . Well, it just never happened.'

He sat back on the stool at the breakfast-bar, and roared with laughter. 'Are you trying to tell me you're still a virgin?' he asked weakly, brushing a tear of mirth from the corner of his eye.

'Yes.'

'Oh, dear.' He shook his head. 'No, I'm sorry, I just don't believe it.'

'Why should I lie about a thing like that?' she demanded furiously.

'I've no idea. Maybe with the mistaken notion of berating me for *my* misdemeanours.'

'There! You don't even deny it!'

He shrugged his wide shoulders in cool indifference. 'Why should I? You only said I wasn't to lay a finger on you. You didn't mention any other names.'

'Well, it's got to stop,' she insisted, goaded beyond endurance. 'I won't stand for any more if it.'

'*You* won't stand for any more of it? What gives *you* the right to start handing out orders?'

'I still own McGill Construction,' she threatened. 'I can still throw you out. I still call the tune around here.'

'Oh, you think so?' She backed away nervously before the menace in his voice. 'Well, maybe it's time I taught you different.'

She tried to side-step out of the kitchen, but he caught her shoulders in a painful grip and pushed her back against the fridge-freezer. She opened her mouth to shriek as she recognised the dark intent in his eyes, but he smothered her cry with a kiss that was an undisguised assault. His lips crushed hers, and his invading tongue plundered ruthlessly into the deepest corners of her mouth.

She struggled wildly to be free, but he was far too strong for her. She felt him loosen the belt of her wrap, and slide his hands inside it to caress her body through the thin silk of her nightdress. Vainly she tried to push him away. 'No... Sam, don't.'

But he only laughed harshly. 'No?' he murmured, his voice low and rough. 'The other night you wanted me—you were practically begging.'

He captured her mouth again, his tongue swirling over the delicate inner membranes, igniting fires inside her that she didn't know how to put out. He sensed her weakness, and ruthlessly took full advantage of it. Her wrap slid to the floor, and he slipped his fingers under the thin straps of her nightdress and pulled them down over her shoulders.

'No... Sam,' she pleaded in a sobbing whisper. 'You promised—we had a deal.'

'The deal's off, as of now,' he growled. 'You can have your divorce—I'll give you any grounds you like. And you can keep your precious company—I don't want any part of it. There's only one thing I want right now.'

The nightdress followed her wrap to the floor, and he crushed her naked body in his arms. His possessive hands stroked down the length of her bare back, and she quivered as she sensed the hard tension of arousal in him. He picked her up, and carried her into the bedroom, and laid her down on the bed, his eyes glittering as he looked down at her.

'Don't fight me, Jess,' he warned tautly. 'I don't want to hurt you.'

He drew her into his arms again, the savagery inside him barely leashed. She trembled as she felt his hands on her body, but she offered no resistance, though his harsh words were echoing in her brain. But as he began to kiss her again every rational thought began to melt away. A warm tide of submissiveness flooded through her, and she wrapped her arms around his neck, curving her slender body invitingly against his.

His breathing was harsh and ragged as he sought the ripe curves of her breasts. His jaw was like sandpaper against her soft skin, and his hot mouth scalded her tender nipples, but she could only surrender to his mastery. And then his hand slid down over the smooth plane of her stomach, to coax apart her slim thighs, and she caught her breath on a gasping sob as she felt the touch of his fingers, light as feathers on velvet.

'Easy,' he murmured, as if soothing a nervous animal.

The magic was weaving around her like a spell; she was responding totally, all constraint forgotten. They were floating in a warm, dark sea of pleasure. But suddenly a sharp pain tore through her, and she couldn't hold back the small cry that broke from her lips.

He looked down at her, a trace of surprise in his smile. 'So truth is stranger than fiction after all,' he mocked softly.

Reality chilled her mind, and she closed her eyes on tears. But it was far too late to stop what was happening. She lay passively beneath him as he took his pleasure, her heart aching for just one loving word. But she got none.

When it was over, he stood up. 'Well, perhaps that'll teach you to take marriage a bit more seriously next time,' he rasped. She stared up at him, hardly able to believe that he really meant what he said. But his eyes were as hard as his voice. 'Goodbye, Jezebel. And good luck—you're probably going to need it.'

With that he was gone. She heard him moving about in his own room, packing, and then she heard the front door slam. Unsteadily she got off the bed, and pattered through to his room. Everything was gone. All that was left of his presence was the jagged stripes he had painted on the wall. She leaned against the door frame, tears coursing freely down her cheeks.

CHAPTER EIGHT

BAD news travels fast. Within a couple of weeks, the whole industry knew that Sam had left McGill Construction, and all Jessica's old problems began to rear their heads. What no one knew was where he had gone. Rumours were flying, but no one knew for certain. Jess was surprised. She had assumed that he would go back to Lisa, and take up his old job in her father's company, but when Lisa returned from her skiing holiday she was alone. After a while she was forced to the conclusion that he had gone abroad.

As some kind of therapy—or maybe it was purgatory—she threw all her energies into work. She advertised for a new chief engineer, but none of the candidates was suitable, so she decided to manage without. It was hard work, wrangling on the phone with suppliers, arguing about rates and bonuses with the unions, angling for contracts. She seemed to be in a permanent state of exhaustion.

'Jess, why don't you go home and rest?' pleaded Fiona when for the second time in one morning she had had a dizzy spell. 'You don't look well.'

'I'm all right,' she snapped impatiently. 'Anyway, how can I go home? I'm due at the Leeds site in a couple of hours—I'm going to be late as it is.'

'Are you sure you're all right to drive?'

'Of course I am. Stop fussing. Where's the file gone? Oh, come *on*, Fiona. I asked you for it half an hour ago.'

'I gave it to you.'

She glanced at her desk. 'Oh...so you did. I'm sorry, Fiona—I don't know what's getting into me these days.'

'You're working far too hard, that's what's the matter.'

Jess sighed ruefully. 'Maybe you're right. Well, it's Easter next weekend—I promise I'll put my feet up then.'

The traffic in London was frustratingly slow, but as soon as she got out on to the motorway she put her foot down, racing down the fast lane, trying to make up time. She didn't notice the police car following her until it was too late.

'Damn!' She punched the steering-wheel in rage as she obeyed their signal to pull over to the hard shoulder. A large policeman got out, and strolled back towards her, ostentatiously taking his time. She pressed the button to lower the window.

'Well, miss,' he drawled. 'You are in a hurry. Got a special date, have you?'

Jess took a deep breath. 'I'm going to a business meeting,' she grated out. 'I'm sorry I was speeding. I'm late.'

He took out his notebook, and regarded his pencil thoughtfully. 'Business, eh? What sort of business would that be?'

'The construction business,' she explained, trying to keep her patience. 'I'm Jessica McGill, of McGill Construction.'

'McGill.' He began to write it down. 'Is that M-a-c, or just M-c?'

'M-c.'

'Ah!'

She had to force herself to curb her rising irritation. It would do no good to lose her temper. 'Look, if you're going to book me for speeding, could you please get on with it?' she pleaded tensely. 'I'm in a hurry.'

'All in good time. I assume this is your car?'

'Of course it is.'

'Would you mind telling me the registration number?'

She recited it, realising with weary resignation that he was going to go through the whole procedure. He took his time, checking her tyres, checking her handbrake, until she was almost at screaming point. At long last he handed her a slip of paper.

'I'll have to report the facts,' he informed her ponderously. 'That offside front tyre is bald as well. You'll need to present your licence and your insurance documents at your local police station, and then you'll be hearing from us in due course.'

'Thank you.'

'Good afternoon. Mind how you go.'

He strolled back to his patrol car, and Jess climbed back into the Porsche, and took a few deep breaths to steady herself before turning the key in the ignition. She drove the rest of the way decorously within the speed limit, and arrived at the site two hours late and in a foul temper.

*   *   *

If there was a law of nature that decreed that everything that could go wrong would go wrong, it was certainly holding sway at McGill Construction. The Sports Complex was finally completed, but so far after the contracted completion date that it represented a substantial net loss; they were called back to do extensive remedial work on a factory extension when it was found that the pre-stressed concrete beams used in the floor were sub-standard.

Jess knew that a lot of the problems were her own fault. Her behaviour was often irrational, her temper uncertain. Life had become an endless bad dream. Over and over she would relive moments with Sam, and think of all the things she could have done or said to make things different between them. But it was too late now, and she was left with only bitter memories.

In May she at last managed to sell the Surrey house, at a knock-down price, and poured the proceeds in to balance the books, though common sense nagged her that she was throwing good money after bad. She knew she was going to have trouble renewing the annual lease on her flat, and the car needed major servicing.

'Jessica, you have to slow down,' Fiona insisted.

'How can I slow down? You know how bad things are. I don't even know if I'm going to be able to pay next month's wages.'

'There are other things more important than that,' insisted Fiona gently.

'What can be more important than that?' she wailed on a rising note of hysteria. 'Don't you understand? I'm going to lose the company.'

'If you keep on like this, you're going to lose the baby.'

Jess stared at her in shock. And then abruptly she burst into tears. She had been trying for months to deny what was happening to her. At first she had put it down to the fact that she wasn't eating properly. Then when the morning sickness and dizzy spells began she had told herself it was due to tension and overwork. Even when her clothes had seemed to start shrinking, she had refused to face the truth. She was nearly five months pregnant.

'Oh, Jessica, I'm so sorry,' soothed Fiona in her kindly way. 'I'm sure it will be all right if you look after yourself from now on. What do they say at the clinic?'

'I haven't been.'

'Not been? But surely you've been to your doctor's?'

'I went once,' she confessed through her tears. 'But when I got in there I just told him I'd been having headaches. He gave me some Valium, and I flushed them down the loo.'

'Well, at least that was a sensible thing to do,' sighed Fiona. 'Now, you're going home, right this minute, and you're going to have a cup of tea and put your feet up. And tomorrow morning you're going right round to see your doctor, or you don't set foot in this office.'

Jess smiled up at her weakly. 'Yes, boss,' she conceded.

Somehow, once she had acknowledged the fact of her pregnancy, it made it easier to let McGill Construction go. Faced with creditors she couldn't pay, she called in the Receiver herself and put the Company into voluntary liquidation.

It was almost a relief that it was all over, though she had been left with next to nothing. Paying the Capital Transfer Tax on Angus's death had absorbed almost everything he had left her beside the firm and the house, and now she had had to sell everything else to try to pay as much as she could of the wages she owed her staff and her debts to the small businessmen who could so easily have gone bankrupt with her.

She had no family to whom she could turn for help, and she had lost contact with most of her friends over the past six months—not that she would have wanted to seek their help anyway. With the lease running out on her flat, she had to go to the local council's housing office to ask for somewhere to live.

It was a difficult and embarrassing interview; she could see what was running through the young woman's mind when she gave her current address—she plainly thought she was dealing with the cast-off mistress of some rich sugar-daddy.

'Well, Miss McGill,' she conceded at last, 'as you're expecting a baby we're obliged to re-house you. It's our normal policy to place homeless persons in bed-and-breakfast accommodation, but I'm afraid landlords aren't very keen to take pregnant women—they cause too much trouble. If you would wait a few moments.'

She was gone for over half an hour. She returned at last with a long white form, and a bunch of keys. Jess's spirits rose. 'I've managed to find a letting for you,' she said, sitting down again. 'I'm afraid you're going to find it a bit of a come-down after where you've been living, but you're lucky to get anything at all. Here are the keys—just sign here. If there are any repairs that need to be done, just let us know.'

The address was in the north end of the Borough—Jess had never heard of it. She signed the form, and handed it back to the woman with a smile. 'Thank you for your help,' she said.

'You haven't seen it yet,' came the inauspicious reply.

She decided to take a taxi from the council offices, although she could ill afford it—but she was afraid she would have trouble finding the address on her own. The streets were unfamiliar, and she gazed in dismay at the evidence of poverty all around.

'Here you are then, love. That's it,' the taxi-driver announced, drawing in to the kerb. Jess stared up at the building with a sinking heart. It was a pre-war tenement block, one of half a dozen around a litter-strewn square, the red-brick walls daubed with the names of the local rival football teams.

'Thank you. Er...do you happen to know where I can catch a bus from here back to the Fulham Road?'

He told her, and even told her what number to catch, adding a cheery 'Good luck,' as she paid her fare.

She stood and gazed up at the ugly building. 'Oh, well, Lumpkin,' she murmured resignedly, patting the round curve of her tummy, 'I guess this is how the other half lives!'

January had brought snow again. Everyone in the bus queue was grumbling at the long wait, and when at last the bus came it was already nearly full. It was a bit of a struggle for Jess to get on, with two heavy bags of shopping and the baby in a sling, but she reflected that it would be even worse when she had to start using a push-chair.

'Melissa, stand up and let the lady sit down.'

'Oh, thank you,' she breathed, smiling down at the woman who had spoken.

'She's been to the dentist, and she's a bit sulky,' the woman confided. 'What a lovely baby. What's his name?'

'Sam.' She stroked the delicate little head that rested against her chest with a proud smile. The baby lifted his head, opened his tiny mouth in a wide yawn, and went back to sleep again.

'Aah. Isn't he good,' purred the woman.

'Except when he wants something,' Jess laughed.

She chatted aimlessly to the woman as the bus jolted and jarred its way along, taking no notice as she was knocked by the shopping-bag of another woman struggling to get off. She had become used to this kind of life now, almost inured to its discomforts and inconveniences. She had little Sam, and the flat that she had managed to turn into a comfortable home for them both.

She never looked back—at least not to her days of wealth. The little money she had had left after the winding-up of the company she had spent on furnishing the flat, and now she was living on Social Security. It wasn't easy, but if she budgeted carefully and allowed herself no extravagance, she could get by.

Her memories of little Sam's father were harder to deal with. She knew she was never going to forget him, and so she tried to be firm with herself, and just allow herself a short time each day to indulge herself with thoughts of the past. The rest of the time, she resolutely got on with the business of living.

'Ah...here's my stop,' she said at last. 'Goodbye. It's been nice talking to you.'

'Goodbye, dear. Mind how you go.'

The bus had emptied out a little, so it wasn't so difficult getting off. She walked briskly up the road and turned the corner, and began to cross the square towards the staircase leading up to her flat.

Half-way across, her footsteps faltered. There was a car parked outside the block—a gleaming dark red XJ6. That in itself was not particularly unusual—some of the ladies of dubious reputation who lived in the block received occasional wealthy callers. Several small boys were hanging around admiring it. Through the tinted windows she could see that the driver was still inside.

No...she was just being stupid. It couldn't possibly be... Not after all this time, just out of the blue like that. She carried on walking, but as she drew level with the car, she hesitated again. The door opened, and the driver got out.

She couldn't speak; her heart was pounding uncomfortably in her chest. She turned away, and walked to the steps, and without a word he followed her. She climbed the two flights to her balcony, and walked along to her front door. She set one of the bags down, took out her key and opened the door, picked up the bag and walked inside, leaving the door open. He closed it behind him.

She went into the kitchen, and put the bags down on the table, and began unpacking them. 'What do you want?' she finally managed to ask.

'I've come to see my son,' he answered in a toneless voice.

She laughed bitterly. 'Your son! I like that! Fat lot you've cared about him so far.'

'I only learned of his existence this morning, when I went to see my solicitor about settling the divorce,' he answered evenly.

Jess couldn't answer. After a moment she lifted the baby carefully out of the sling, and put him into Sam's arms, and walked past him into the sitting-room, to stare out of the window. 'Where have you been?' she asked at last.

'Back to San Marcos.'

'You seem to have done quite well for yourself,' she remarked tartly.

'Very well,' he confirmed. 'Things have settled down again now. The new government were very anxious to do business with me. I finished the contracts I was working on when the trouble started, and several more besides.'

Jess shrugged helplessly. 'Congratulations,' she said. Bravely she turned back to face him. 'Well, we can get the divorce sorted out now, and then forget all about each other again,' she added briskly.

'Not quite.' He had sat down, with the baby in his arms. The baby's tiny fist was wrapped tightly around his finger. 'We've got this little fellow to think about now.'

Jess felt a sudden surge of panic. 'W...what do you mean?' she demanded.

He cast a disparaging eye around the room, noting the damp patch on the wall where the pointing outside was crumbling away, and the uneven fit of the door. 'Is this any sort of place to bring up a child?' he asked.

'The council said I can get a transfer when I've been here a year,' she told him, trying to sound as if she believed it herself.

He laughed drily. 'Do you really think there's much hope of that? Look out there—how long have those people been waiting to move somewhere better? They've put you here, and now they'll forget all about you—you're just another one-parent family.'

His words cut her with their truth. She turned to stare bleakly out of the window again. Across the road, a group of small boys—no more than five or six years old—were hurling bricks at a window in one of the empty flats. Their piping voices were raised in excitement—but the language they were using would have been worthy of a bunch of navvies.

Was this all she could offer little Sam? 'I...I might be able to afford to buy a little place of my own eventually,' she stammered. 'I was thinking of going back to work. Modelling, perhaps...or I could try to get a job as some sort of personal assistant. I'm sure my business experience could come in useful.'

'And what do you propose to do with my son while you're doing that?' he enquired, menacingly soft.

She turned round again to confront him in fury. 'Well, what about you?' she demanded. 'You can afford to run a nice expensive car—why don't you help out a bit?'

His eyes were cold. 'Oh, I thought it would come to that,' he sneered. 'Looking for a meal-ticket, are you?'

'No!' Angry tears sprang to her eyes. 'Give him back to me,' she cried, crossing the room swiftly. He didn't argue, and she retreated back to the window, hugging the baby possessively.

'You can have him for now,' he said, a thread of warning in his voice, 'but if I'm not convinced that you can look after him properly, I'll get my lawyers on to it, and believe me, I'll use every trick in the book to make sure that I get awarded custody of him.'

She stared at him in horror. 'Don't be ridiculous,' she retorted, her voice shaking. 'No judge in the world would take him away from me.'

'No?' He lifted one eyebrow in cool scepticism. 'You'd better be very sure of that. Your past history might not look too good to court, you know. And don't forget, I'm a rich man again now—I can afford the best lawyers. And with all due respect to your legal-aid hack...' He left the threat hanging in the air.

'You bastard,' she spat. 'I hate you. Don't you dare try to take my baby away.' She sank weakly into an armchair. Surely Sam couldn't get custody...? And yet...there was just enough truth in what he had said to make her uneasy.

She cuddled the baby in her arms, resting her cheek against his tiny head and stroking the fine silky hair—so dark, just like his father's. If she lost him... The tears trickled unchecked down her cheeks.

There was a long silence, and when at last Sam spoke again there was a different note in his voice.

'It would really break your heart to lose him, wouldn't it?' She didn't even bother to answer such a fatuous question. 'I'm sorry,' he said after a while. 'I didn't expect to find that you cared about him so much.'

'I'm his mother,' she answered tautly. 'Of course I care about him.'

'I'm his father, Jess,' he reminded her with quiet insistence. 'I care about him too.'

'You!' She glared at him scornfully. 'You just walked in here ten minutes ago. Where were you when I was expecting him, and didn't have anywhere to live? Where were you when he was born, and he was so tiny they had to put him in an incubator for the first week?'

He ran a hand back through his hair. 'I didn't know, Jess. I was out of the country...'

'You didn't want to know,' she snarled. 'You raped me, and then...'

'Oh, come on! If that was rape...!'

Her cheeks flamed scarlet as she remembered. 'Well, you just went off,' she mumbled.

'I walked out before I was kicked out,' he returned, an ironic inflection in his voice. 'I broke our deal, remember?'

She refused to meet his eyes. Somehow he still had that knack of coaxing her when she wanted to be angry. 'Oh, all right,' she conceded with a show of reluctance. 'I suppose it was my fault too, the way things turned out.'

He smiled. 'We don't have to fight over him, you know. There is an alternative.' She glanced up at him enquiringly. 'We could get back together.'

She laughed, not sure if he was joking. 'Us? We fight like cat and dog,' she protested.

'We've got a good reason to try not to now,' he pointed out reasonably. 'Come on, I'll give it my best shot if you will. I want my son to have both his parents.'

Jess hesitated, her mind in turmoil. Certainly it was much better for a child to grow up in a proper family— so long as that family wasn't constantly disrupted by rows and hostility. Maybe she ought at least to give it a try... But her heart quaked at the thought of living with Sam again. The past year had done nothing to change the way she felt about him, and now that he was sitting here, so close...

'Look, I...I need a little time to think about it,' she said. 'Plus I haven't had my lunch yet, and nor has Sam. Have you?'

'No.'

'Well, I can't offer you much, I'm afraid. Will cheese on toast be all right? And I'm afraid my coffee's only instant.'

'That'll be fine. Thank you.'

She made her escape to the kitchen, and busied herself with putting the kettle on and making Sam's lunch. But instead of rationally weighing up the pros and cons of Sam's suggestion, she found that her mind had flipped back in time, to the first meal she had cooked for him—that gargantuan breakfast on the morning before their wedding, when he had arrived so unexpectedly early, and caught her apparently *in flagrante delicto* with Mark.

She smiled to herself. He had certainly taken over her life. Could it really be that they had lived together for less than six weeks? It seemed as if it had been much longer. But then of course he had left her with a reminder of that brief time that would last for the rest of her life.

She loaded the mugs and plates on to a tray, and carried them carefully through to the sitting-room. On the threshold she paused. Sam was cradling his son in his strong arms, and the baby was gazing up at his face with huge, solemn eyes. An odd little constriction tightened around her heart. He was holding the baby so gently, talking to him and playing with his fluffy rabbit, making him gurgle.

He glanced up as she came in, a question in his eyes. Quickly she crossed to the table, and set down the tray. 'You'd better put him in his baby-seat while we're eating,' she said over her shoulder. 'He likes to be able to sit up and watch what's going on.'

'OK. Come on then, little 'un.' He lifted the baby up, and held him over the seat. 'No, put your feet through there... No, look...'

Jess smiled tolerantly at his efforts. 'Give him to me,' she chaffed him lightly. 'Come on, Lumpkin. In you go.' She slid the baby into the seat, and buffed his rosy cheek. 'There, it's easy when you know how.'

'I've got a lot to learn,' he agreed with a grin.

Jess's eyes flashed with anger at his assumption that she would accede to his threats and cajolery. She sat down at the table, and peeled the top off her yoghurt.

'You still don't eat much,' he remarked as he tucked into his own meal.

'I eat well enough,' she countered defensively.

He lifted one questioning eyebrow. 'You're sure it isn't that you can't afford more?' he enquired.

'Money is tight,' she conceded reluctantly. 'But I manage.'

'I don't suppose it's easy.'

'No, it isn't.' She met his eyes with a cool, level gaze. 'But I'm not looking for a meal-ticket.'

A wry expression crossed his face. 'All right— perhaps that wasn't a fair comment.' She inclined her head in acceptance of his apology. 'How did you come down to this, Jess?' he asked. 'I could hardly believe it when I saw where you were living.'

She shrugged her shoulders. 'You were right—I should never have tried to run the company myself, but I was too stupid and pig-headed to admit it. It went bankrupt last summer, and I lost my shirt, as the saying goes.'

'But surely...wasn't there anyone who could help you?'

'Who? I've no family to speak of—unless you count some cousins in Scotland that I've never seen. Or were you thinking of one of my old friends? Lisa, perhaps?' she added, unable to keep the edge of sarcasm from her voice.

He had the decency to look faintly discomfited. 'No, I suppose not...'

'Anyway,' she went on brightly, 'while I've been hitting rock-bottom, you seem to have been on the up-and-up. So what happens now? Are you planning to stay in England?'

'Yes.' He finished his meal, and leaned back in his seat to drink his coffee. 'I'm starting several contracts here over the next couple of months. I've still got quite a lot of work abroad, but I intend to make my base here now, and set up a permanent office.'

'"Ryder Construction"?' she asked, an ironic twist in her smile.

'Yes.'

She laughed in bitter self-mockery. 'We seem to have swapped places,' she remarked drily.

'So it seems.'

She realised she was twirling her spoon between her fingers in a way that betrayed her nervousness, and stopped abruptly. 'So where are you living?' she asked.

'At the moment I'm staying in a small hotel just round the corner from Holland Park. But I want to look for a house when I get enough time.'

She nodded, reading the question in his eyes again.

'Well?' he prompted gently. 'Have you made up your mind yet? Or do you still want more time to think about it?'

'No, I...all right.' Her heart was thudding. 'You're right,' she agreed, trying to keep her voice cool, 'it would be better for little Sam. The least we can do is give it a try. And...and if it doesn't work out, say after three months, we could still go ahead with the divorce. OK?'

He nodded agreement. 'Very well. Three months— that seems fair enough.'

'Right. Well, I'd better get his lunch now, and then I can start sorting out my stuff. I don't have a lot to pack.'

'What time shall I come to fetch you?' he asked.

She shrugged. 'When you like. I only need a couple of hours.'

'OK. Shall we say five o'clock then?'

'Five o'clock.' She managed a reasonable attempt at a smile.

He crouched down in front of the baby. 'Have you got a goodbye kiss for Daddy, then?' he asked. The baby chuckled, and waved his arms excitedly. Sam laughed, and dropped a kiss on the end of his button nose. 'Bye-bye, cherub. See you soon.'

Jess showed him to the front door. She couldn't quite make herself lift her eyes to his face. 'Well, I'll see you later, then,' she murmured.

'You will.'

She closed the door behind him, and leaned her back against it, letting go of her breath in a long sigh. How often had she dreamed that one day Sam would come back to claim her? But in her dreams he had always swept in, full of declarations of remorse and undying love for her. Reality wasn't quite so pretty.

A loud bawl cut across her thoughts, and she smiled wryly. 'All right, Lumpkin. I'm coming,' she promised, and hurried into the kitchen to make up the baby's feed.

CHAPTER NINE

JESS didn't have a lot to pack. She sorted little Sam's clothes, and stowed them carefully into a couple of large plastic bags, and packed her own things in a plastic dustbin-liner—she didn't have any suitcases. She didn't have many clothes—she had put on a little weight since before her pregnancy, and few of her old things still fitted her.

She packed the food from the kitchen in a couple of cartons, and took them round to her next-door neighbour, who accepted them with delight. Then she busied herself with dusting, making sure everything was left clean and tidy.

She was ready long before five o'clock. Little Sam was bouncing contentedly in his baby-seat, gurgling and trying to play with his toes, untroubled by her nervousness. When there came a knock at the door she jumped as if it had been a gun-shot.

She could see Sam's large frame through the frosted glass as she walked down the hall. Taking one deep, steadying breath, she opened the door, and forced a bright smile. 'Hello. You're right on time,' she greeted him, hoping he wouldn't notice the tremor in her voice.

'Are you ready?' he asked pleasantly.

'Of course. I've put his steriliser and everything in his bath—can you carry that? I'll bring the rest.'

'Right. What about his cot?'

'Oh, he still sleeps in his carry-cot.' She sensed the start of a frown. 'Oh, he likes it,' she assured him quickly. 'They often feel more secure in a small cot. I was going to get a proper one when he gets a bit bigger—the Social have given me the money.'

'I see.' His voice was expressionless, but it was evident that he didn't like the idea of his son sleeping in a second-hand cot bought with Social Security benefit.

They managed to get most of the bulkier things in the boot of the car, and then went back for the bags of clothing. Jess settled little Sam in his carry-cot, making sure he had his precious blue fluffy rabbit, and then Sam picked it up and carried it carefully down to the car.

Quickly Jess checked that she hadn't forgotten anything, and that all the windows were closed. Then she turned off the electricity, making a note of what was on the meter. She stood for a moment, looking around the sitting-room. Strangely, she was sadder to leave here than she had been to leave the far more comfortable flat she had had in the Fulham Road. She had found a sort of contentment here. With a small sigh she swung her handbag on to her shoulder, and somehow managed to pick up the rest of the plastic bags.

Her progress along the balcony was slow. Several of her neighbours had come out to see what was happening. She didn't really mind—she knew that in most cases it was friendly concern rather than crude nosiness.

'You're off then?' the woman next door asked kindly.

'Yes. Keep an eye on my flat, would you, until I can settle up the tenancy?'

'You're not coming back then?'

'I don't know. I don't think so,' she answered cautiously.

'Who's your chap?' asked one of the others enviously. 'You kept pretty quiet about him.'

'He's my husband.' She took a deep breath. 'We're going to give it another try.'

The women nodded understanding. 'Oh, yes. For the sake of the baby. It's always worth trying. No one wants to be on their own with a baby.'

'No. Well, goodbye.' She was becoming a little agitated, looking over the balcony. Sam had put the carry-cot on the back seat of the car. If he should drive away with it . . .

'Goodbye, love. And good luck,' they called after her as she hurried down the steps.

She tucked the bags in carefully around the carry-cot, wedging them tightly so that it wouldn't move around if the car braked or swerved suddenly. 'We ought to get a proper safety-harness for it,' she mused.

'I'll have one fitted tomorrow,' Sam agreed at once.

Jess glanced at him thoughtfully as she slid into the passenger seat and fastened her seat-belt. He certainly seemed intent on making sure his son was properly cared for. He probably felt guilty that he had left him to have such a difficult start in life.

But he had made it only too clear that his concern was all for the child—he wouldn't have cared what happened to her. If this trial reconciliation didn't work out, would he really try to take him away from her?

She bit her lip. Why did he have to come back, and disrupt her life like this?

She turned to look back at the flats as the car swung out into the main road. She ought to be glad to be leaving that life behind her. But once again, Sam was in control. And again she would have to hide her heart away, somewhere safe where it wouldn't get broken.

It was only a short drive. They drew up outside a small, smart-looking hotel, in a quiet street close to Holland Park. The doorman and the receptionist glanced up in amazement as they entered, Sam holding the carry-cot, Jess carrying three bulging plastic bags. Suddenly she felt all too conscious of her cheap clothes.

'Get the porter to bring the rest of my wife's things up to my suite, will you?' Sam requested pleasantly, increasing their surprise.

'Of course, Mr Ryder. Right away.' The receptionist leaned forward to peer into the carry-cot. 'Oh, isn't he sweet! How old is he?' she asked.

'Three months,' Jess told her.

'Ahh! Is there anything you need for him, Mrs Ryder?'

'Well...it would be helpful if I could come down to the kitchen and make up his feed. He's going to wake up any minute.' She smiled in rueful expectation.

'Of course. Here—let me give you a hand with those things.'

'Oh...thank you so much. I don't want to be any trouble,' murmured Jess, relinquishing one of the bags to the helpful girl. It seemed strange to be called Mrs Ryder—even during the weeks she and Sam had lived together, everyone had continued to call her Miss

McGill, and she had gone on using that name ever since.

And she had forgotten what it was like to be pampered. Suddenly she felt as though she were a different person from the one who had woken up that morning. But whether she was going to enjoy being that person was another matter, she reflected wryly, slanting a wary glance up at Sam as he stood aside for her to step into the lift.

The suite was luxurious: deep leather armchairs, and a dark green carpet with a velvet-smooth pile, matching the satin curtains at the long windows. Beyond the sitting-room she glimpsed a small lobby, where she guessed were the bedrooms and bathroom. She glanced around, uncomfortably aware of the contrast with her own recent life-style.

Sam set the carry-cot down carefully on a low onyx coffee-table, and turned as the porter came in, carrying the baby-bath and plastic dustbin-liners with as much dignity as if they had been the finest leather luggage. 'Thank you. Just put them here,' he requested, slipping the man a discreet tip.

'I'd better fix the baby's feed right away,' said Jess, glad at the excuse to escape for a few minutes. 'Once he wakes up, all hell will be let loose if it isn't ready.' She gathered up the things quickly, and followed the receptionist down to the hotel's kitchen, where the chef was most obliging in letting her use his facilities.

She could hear little Sam's furious cries the moment she stepped out of the lift. She felt a little guilty as she hurried along the plush corridor—the advent of a tiny baby had certainly shattered the elegant quiet of the hotel!

Sam was trying anxiously to soothe his son, and was plainly perturbed by his lack of success. His eyes lit with relief when he saw her. 'Ah—here's your mama with your dinner,' he told him. 'Now perhaps you'll stop that dreadful racket!'

Jess smiled. 'He knows it's quite unnecessary,' she said as she took him from Sam's arms. 'He just does it to let me know he's there, don't you, Lumpkin?' She settled herself in one of the other armchairs, and put the baby's bib round his neck. 'And you can stop kicking me—I know you're the best centre-forward England's ever produced.'

Blissful silence reigned as the tiny mouth closed hungrily on the bottle. Jess relaxed back in the chair with a sigh. She always enjoyed feeding-times—she seemed to share in the baby's contentment. Even with Sam's eyes watching her, she felt happy.

'You didn't try breast-feeding him then?' Sam asked.

'I did for the first two months,' she told him, too comfortable to feel annoyed at his questioning. 'But I had to have antibiotics just before Christmas to clear up a bad throat, so I put him on to the bottle. He doesn't seem to mind.'

'And you're not using proper nappies.'

She sighed. 'I couldn't have got them dry at the flat,' she explained patiently. 'All the washing lines are vandalised, and anyway I was told the first day I moved in that if I put any washing out it would get stolen.'

'Oh.' He nodded, apparently accepting her explanation.

Suddenly Jess was seized with curiosity to know more about Sam's history. He had never mentioned his family at all. 'I was thinking about getting him christened,' she mused, trying to broach the subject in a roundabout way, 'only I didn't really know who to ask to be godparents.' She glanced up at him warily. 'What about you? Do you have any brothers or sisters?'

'Yes. But they all live in Australia.'

'Oh?' she prompted delicately.

'They emigrated out there with my stepfather when I was fifteen.'

'You didn't go with them?'

'No. I went to live with my father instead.' He paused, and then went on without further prompting. 'He died a few years ago. It's a shame—he'd have liked to see his grandson—he was fond of kids.' There was a hint of sadness in his voice, and Jess didn't like to probe further. But she was glad that she had learned that much, at least. She felt it helped her to understand him a little more.

He didn't want to risk being deprived of his son, as his father had been. And perhaps he hadn't got on with his stepfather, and didn't like the idea of one being inflicted upon little Sam—not that she had had the least intention of doing so. If they fought over custody, one of them would lose—this way, they had achieved a sort of compromise. As for the rest of it... no, she wouldn't think about that just yet.

Little Sam had finished his bottle, and was gurgling with satisfaction, kicking his strong little legs. 'Right, young man,' said Jess, sitting him forward to bring up his wind, 'it's a nice bath for you, and then bed, eh?'

'You're going to bath him now?' asked Sam.

'Yes—if that's all right?'

'Of course—keep him to his routine. Can I help?'

Jess laughed. 'What, help bath him?' He nodded. 'Certainly—if you want to. I warn you, though, you're likely to get very wet.'

He grinned. 'I won't mind that.'

It was a lot of fun, kneeling on the floor of the luxurious bathroom, laughing at the slippery little body as he kicked in his bath, drenching them both. 'You were wrong, you know,' declared Sam proudly. 'He isn't going to be a footballer—he's going to be a Channel-swimmer.'

'Oh, no,' Jess insisted. 'He's bound to be a foot-baller. One of my uncles used to play in the Scottish league.'

'Well, a distant cousin of mine has swum the Channel,' he countered, 'and he's bound to take after my side of the family.'

'How do you figure that out?'

'Well, he looks like me. Look at him—my nose, my chin. Come on then, Lumpkin. "Drowning Daddy" time's over.' He lifted the baby out of his bath, and wrapped him up in the towel to dry him.

Jess laughed softly. 'I never thought I'd see you playing big daddy,' she teased.

He looked up at her seriously. 'I didn't think you'd make much of a mother,' he remarked, 'but I was wrong.'

Suddenly she felt tears rising inside her. It was so easy for them to enjoy being parents, and pretend for a few moments that everything was all right. But nothing was right, nothing had changed—in a sense it was worse than ever. 'I forgot his clean nappy,' she said, making her escape.

They had dinner sent up to their suite, because Jess would not leave the baby alone there while they went down to the dining-room. Then she curled up in one of the armchairs to get on with her knitting—she was making little Sam a pair of blue dungarees. Sam sat opposite her, working his way through a long report.

It was a pleasant, peaceful evening—only the clicking of her knitting needles disturbed the silence. But night was coming, and she could no longer ignore the anxious questions in the back of her mind. Would Sam be expecting her to sleep with him? He hadn't said so, but she couldn't believe that he didn't have that intention.

At last she yawned and stretched, and put down her knitting. 'Well, it's time for little Sam's last feed,' she said. 'I'd better go and fix it before he wakes up.'

Sam glanced up at her. 'What do I do if he starts screaming again?' he asked with a crooked smile.

'He won't. He never does that at this feed, for some reason. Then he just goes straight back down again, and usually sleeps right through the night.'

He grinned. 'That's good.'

Jess felt that quivering of nervous tension inside her again. 'I won't be a minute,' she said, and hurried down to the kitchen. She seemed to be all fingers and thumbs as she made up the feed. She spilled half the milk powder on the floor, and had to find a dust-pan and brush to sweep it up.

When she got back upstairs, Sam had brought the baby into the sitting-room, and was playing with him on his lap. 'Look,' he announced proudly, 'he can almost stand already!'

Jess smiled. 'Of course. He's very clever. He can blow lovely raspberries, too, can't you, Lumpkin?'

'Can you?' Sam asked the baby solemnly. 'Show Daddy.' The baby put out one dimpled hand, and smacked him clumsily on the nose. Sam chuckled with laughter.

As Jess watched, she felt that odd little lump in her throat again. Sam was revealing a soft centre she had never dreamed he possessed. He would make a good father. 'Do you want to feed him?' she asked. He glanced up at her, his eyes betraying a hint of apprehension that made her laugh. 'It isn't difficult. Here you are...oh, wait a minute, he needs a bib or he'll dribble all down his sleeping-suit.'

Little Sam didn't seem to mind in the least being fed by this new person in his life. He gazed up at his father with huge solemn eyes, and as the bottle slowly emptied he began to fall into a placid sleep.

'That's enough,' said Jess. 'Now you just have to get his wind up, and he can go down again.'

'You'd better do that then,' said Sam. 'I've still got my L-plates on.'

She took the precious bundle carefully from his arms, and lifted the tiny head against her shoulder. 'Ah, come to mama then,' she murmured, loving the warm, milky smell of him. 'Pass me that towel, Sam. I don't want him to be sick on me.'

The baby was already fast asleep as they laid him in his cot. Jess settled him gently, and stood gazing down at him. He looked so cosy and peaceful, wrapped up in his blanket, his long dark lashes shadowing his rosy cheeks, and his blue fluffy rabbit standing guard.

She was all too aware of Sam standing close beside her, and a strange little ache had begun deep inside her. Her body seemed to have a will of its own. An angry pride reminded her of all the heartbreak she had suffered at his hands, but the longing to lie in his arms, to feel his kisses, was almost unbearable.

She crept softly from the room, and he followed her, closing the door quietly behind him. For a moment she hesitated in the lobby, looking up at him with wide, apprehensive eyes. When he touched her she started as if a shock of electricity had jolted through her.

'What's wrong?' he asked.

'I . . . I . . .'

He drew her gently into his arms. 'I think it's time for you and me to go to bed now, don't you?' he asked.

'T . . . together?' she stammered, staring at the button of his shirt.

He laughed softly. 'Of course together. It isn't going to work any other way, is it, Jess?'

Some compulsion stronger than the force of gravity made her lift her eyes to meet his. He was smiling down at her in quizzical amusement, challenging her to deny his words. 'I . . . I think I'd like a bath first,' she managed to say.

'Whatever you like.'

He let her go without demur, and she made her escape quickly to the bathroom, locking the door safely behind her. So it had come to the crunch—and she knew that she wasn't going to be able to refuse him. With shaking hands she reached out to turn on the bath-taps.

It was sheer luxury to be able to run the bath deep with hot water and not have to worry about the electricity bill, and to be able to strip off her clothes in a warm bathroom. She sank down into the water, letting it lap over her breasts. It would be nice if she had some of the expensive perfumed oil she used to use—lately she had had to make do with baby-oil to keep her skin soft.

She had to admit, wealth had its advantages. The best things in life might be free, but many of the simple comforts had been beyond her tight purse for a long time—the succulent lamb cutlets she had had for dinner, the peace of mind to be able to relax in the evening without being disturbed by a nearby domestic brawl or worse.

Sam was offering her a lot. Maybe what he was asking in return wasn't so much after all. If she was going to enjoy the privileges of being his wife, she must be ready to fulfil the duties too. A small shimmer of heat ran through her, and she ran her hands down the length of her body. Duties . . . Memories swirled in her brain, and she closed her eyes, her breath warm on her lips.

She was reluctant to leave her dreams, apprehensive of the reality, but she would have to face it sooner or later. As the water began to get cold she climbed out of the bath, and dried herself briskly on one of the hotel's huge fluffy towels.

She still had a little of the perfume Sam had bought her the previous Christmas, so she dabbed a little at her throat and between her breasts, and then brushed her hair vigorously, so that the rich auburn lights gleamed as it curled around her shoulders.

It was a shame she only had the cheap cotton night-dress she had bought from the market. It would have given her more confidence to have been able to drift out in a cloud of satin and lace. It wasn't even pretty—it was a jokey nightshirt in red and white stripes, with buttons down the front. But she couldn't go and climb into bed with nothing on—she didn't have the nerve.

She took her time tidying up the bathroom—dammit, she couldn't postpone this for ever! Taking a deep breath, she opened the door, and stepped out into the bedroom. It was empty, but the bed had been turned down, and . . .

'You took your time.' She turned sharply, her heart leaping into her throat. He was standing in the doorway, now wearing only a dark blue cotton kimono. 'I used the bathroom down the hall. I thought you were never going to come out.' He laughed in faint mockery as he let his eyes wander over her. 'You look more like Wee Willy Winkie than Queen Jezebel,' he remarked.

She felt a blush rising to her cheeks, and lowered her eyes, unable to meet his gaze. Her mouth was dry, and her heart was racing out of control.

'Come here,' he said softly.

Slowly—very slowly—she crossed the room. He reached out one hand, and twirled his finger around a long curl of her auburn hair.

'You're still the most beautiful woman I ever saw,' he murmured smokily.

A tingle of nervous anticipation shimmered through her. She felt the brush of his lips on her temples, across her quivering eyelids, and then he drew her into his arms, curving her close against him as his mouth sought hers. His hands curled into her hair to hold her still as his sensuous tongue coaxed apart her lips, swirling languorously over the sweet inner membranes, stirring the embers of a fire that had never died since he had first kindled it all those months ago.

The kiss became deeper, ravishing every corner of her mouth, and his hand trailed slowly down the shivering cleft of her spine, arching her body against the hard length of his and making her intimately aware of how much he wanted her. As the racing of her blood dizzied her she had to wrap her arms around his neck, clinging to him as if she were afraid that she would fall.

His hand began to move again, roving up over the slender curve of her hip, past her waist...and then his thumb brushed up to the full undercurve of her breast. His mouth broke from hers, and she could hear the harsh drag of his breathing, as ragged as her own, as his fingers cupped possessively around the aching swell of her breast, and the pad of his thumb brushed teasingly across the taut head of her nipple beneath the thin cotton fabric of her nightshirt.

He lifted his head and looked down at her, his eyes dark and blazing with barely restrained hunger. 'You're even lovelier than I remembered,' he murmured huskily. 'You've filled out in all the right places.'

'I've had a baby,' she reminded him in a shaking voice.

Her words seemed to hover in the air between them. She had had *his* baby. Nothing could bind them more closely. His hand was shaking with the urgency of his desire as it slid down over her body, exploring the new, softer contours. Then he took a pace back, and began to unfasten the buttons down the front of her nightshirt.

With slow deliberation he unfastened every button, and slid the fabric back over her shoulders, and let it fall to the floor. The blush seemed to spread all over her body as he looked at her. Every second was timeless. She could have been a statue, a naked Venus, except for a nervous pulse that fluttered in the hollow of her throat.

He put out his hand again, and stroked it over the smooth curve of her hip. She seemed to stop breathing as his touch moved upwards, slowly, as if savouring every changing texture of her skin. Slowly, up over the proud swell of her breast, until his thumb found again the raspberry puckering of her nipple.

At that exquisite touch she let go her breath in a gasping sob, swaying as weakness filled her body. He reached out and drew her to him, cradling her head against his hard chest as he continued to fondle her aching breast, reducing her to a state of helpless abandon.

Just at the moment when she thought she could no longer stand, even with his support, he scooped her up in his arms and carried her over to lay her on the bed. He stood for a moment looking down at her, the heat of his gaze caressing every naked curve, and she reached up for him urgently, needing to feel the touch of his body against hers. In a swift movement he shrugged off his cotton kimono, and sank into her arms.

Any doubts she had known evaporated with his gentleness. This was the lover she had dreamed about through all the long lonely nights, caressing her with a slow hand, taking time to arouse her at every stage, until she was melting in the glowing warmth as he coaxed her closer and closer to the fire.

She felt ashamed of her own lack of experience, longing to caress him with a fraction of the skill with which he was caressing her, but he put her hands back on the pillow. 'No. Just let me enjoy you,' he whispered.

'But . . .'

'There'll be time for more advanced lessons another time.'

So she lay back and let the pleasure wash over her, wave upon wave, like some warm, gentle sea. She shivered with delight as his teeth nibbled lightly at the lobe of her ear, and her spine curved in sensuous pleasure like a cat as his hot mouth moved on down, over the slender column of her throat to savour the creamy fulness of her breasts.

She moved beneath him in shameless invitation, offering him the erotic morsel of one tender pink nipple, and a strange, animal cry broke from her lips as she felt the heat of his mouth, the sinuous roughness of his tongue, tormenting the sensitive nerve endings with a delicious agony.

Her body was filled with a primitive longing so powerful that it almost frightened her. She clung to

Sam, glorying in his hard, muscular strength. He was there, soothing and arousing her with a kiss, swirling his tongue languorously into the deepest parts of her mouth, lifting her pliant body into his arms.

But even as he reassured her, his hand was stroking down over her slim thighs, coaxing them gently apart. She could only surrender. His touch was soft, magical, seeking deep into the secret heart of intimate pleasure, and the ecstasy throbbed through her whole body.

She moved beneath him in total surrender, aching for his possession. Her responsiveness had aroused him to a point where he was barely in control, and when he took her it was with such urgency that she gasped in shock. But the next instant a pulsating wave of heat surged through her, and his mouth claimed hers to complete the union.

She was one with him, her body moving instinctively to the driving rhythm of his as they rode the wild waves of the storm, lightning in her veins and thunder in her ears, and tears flooding her eyes like rain.

When at last it was over, he lifted his weight from her, and fell heavily on to the pillow beside her, with a grunt of deep contentment. 'There,' he murmured, 'That wasn't so bad, was it?'

She looked at him in surprise. A teasing smile was curving his mouth. 'No,' she conceded carefully, 'it wasn't so bad.'

He chuckled with laughter, and drew her into his arms. 'At least you can't try to pretend that I raped you this time,' he taunted. 'Not that it was rape last time. Was it?'

He was looking into her eyes, demanding an answer. 'No,' she confessed, 'it wasn't.'

He sighed with satisfaction, and settled her down comfortably against his shoulder. 'I'm glad to hear you admit it,' he murmured sleepily.

Her heart ached as all the love she had ever felt for him was rekindled. But even though she longed to share it with him, she knew that for her own protection she must keep it locked up and secret. He already had one powerful hold over her, through her nagging fear of losing her tiny son. If he should ever suspect that she had another tender spot in her heart he would walk all over her.

CHAPTER TEN

JESS opened her eyes to find Sam leaning over her. 'Good morning, Mrs Ryder,' he greeted her, his husky tone telling her exactly what was on his mind. She backed away from him instinctively, feeling far too vulnerable to repeat the experience of last night.

'No, Sam, please. Not again . . .'

But he caught her, and spread-eagled her on the bed, half crushing her with his weight. 'Yes, again,' he whispered roughly. 'And again and again and again. You surely didn't think I'd be satisfied with only once?'

He bent his head over her, and she felt the sensuous swirl of his tongue around the delicate shell of her ear. She couldn't hide the tremor of response that ran through her. He chuckled softly. 'And don't even try to pretend that you aren't going to enjoy it,' he murmured. 'Not after last night. And that was only a beginning. Once you learn the moves you're going to be sensational.'

Jess slanted him a nervous glance. Last night was only a beginning . . . ? The beginning of what? she wondered wildly. Already he was raising her temperature by several degrees, and he was only nibbling her ear!

The nibbling began to move south, lingering in the sensitive hollows of her throat, and then seeking the hilly territory further on. She shivered as his un-

shaven cheek rasped over her silken skin. Anticipation was building a delicious tension inside her as
her body remembered the pleasures she had enjoyed.
She moved beneath him invitingly, and he laughed at
her eagerness.

'There, you see? I always knew you were a wanton
hussy. Just like your namesake.'

'My name's Jessica, not Jezebel,' she reminded him
tartly.

'Jezebel,' he murmured, his hot mouth devouring
her. 'Jezebel, Jezebel, Jezebel.'

She tried again to pull away from him, angry that
he was finding all her weaknesses and forcing her to
play the role he had cast her in. But he held her down,
and continued his voyage of discovery, ignoring her
diminishing protests. He paused to dally around her
navel, sending hot little thrills scudding along her
spine, and then he moved on further, into tropical
regions.

She was completely lost, melting in the heat, following him blindly. Her body stretched in languorous
pleasure like a cat, and she moaned softly. He worked
his way slowly right down to her toes, nibbling them
one by one, and then back up again, taking in several
interesting diversions on the way. When at last he
gazed down into her eyes again, he saw there only
willing surrender.

But then he wrapped his arms around her, and
rolled on to his back, drawing her over to lie on top
of him. 'Now it's your turn,' he announced.

She stared at him in shock, a scarlet blush rising
to her cheeks. 'What . . . ?'

'Go on. Exactly the way I did. It's about time you did some work instead of just lying back and enjoying it!'

He gave her one tender kiss to encourage her on her way, and then she began, feeling like a harlot but excited beyond belief by the feel of smooth, hard muscle and tough, tanned skin. She twirled her fingertips through the rough dark hair that was scattered all over his body, and pressed her lips to places where his pulse beat strongly beneath his skin, so that his very life-force seemed to thrill right through her.

And when she got to his toes, she made an interesting discovery. He had very ticklish feet. She laughed as he squealed in protest, teasing him with her eyes, and he reared up in mock fury. 'Right, madam,' he warned. 'You're going to pay for that!'

She dodged away, but he caught her swiftly, and threw her down across the bed, taking her with an urgency that inflamed her own desire to white heat. She cried out as the pleasure flooded through her in mounting waves of intensity, until she felt as though she were exploding into a million shivering crystal pieces, ten thousand degrees Fahrenheit.

When it was over she lay dazed in his arms, exhausted, her breathing ragged and her heartbeat pounding as it slowed at last to its normal steady beat. When she opened her eyes she saw that he was watching her, his eyes smiling as she had never seen them before.

But a small voice in the back of her head whispered caution. That he found her beautiful, that he enjoyed making love to her, didn't necessarily mean that he felt any deeper emotion. Maybe, given time... But for the moment, she reminded herself grimly, it was just sex. He had just returned from abroad, and he hadn't yet had the opportunity to set up any liaisons. So for the time being it suited his convenience to make his wife into his mistress. But how long would it be before that entertainment palled?

She sighed, and heaved herself with some difficulty into a sitting position. 'Well, I'd better go and see to your son,' she suggested, 'before he decides to wake the whole of Kensington and Chelsea.'

Life slipped into a new pattern. Jess couldn't deny that it was pleasant, in spite of the minor inconveniences of living in a hotel with a small baby. She had no money worries—Sam opened a bank account for her, and insisted that she buy herself some nice clothes.

'I want to be able to take my wife out and show her off,' he declared. 'You can't dine at the Café de Paris in something you bought off a market stall.'

Jess pouted, her eyes laughing. 'You're supposed to say I'd look sensational in a paper sack,' she protested teasingly.

He gave her an intimate little pat on the behind. 'You look your best when you're wearing nothing at all,' he murmured huskily, 'but I'm not taking you out to dinner like that, either.'

He also persuaded her to take on an au pair to help look after little Sam. They were very lucky to find a solid and sensible German girl called Helga, who had spent the previous summer looking after her sister's small baby because her sister had been very ill. She knew how to undertake all the routine tasks without taking over the mother's place, and she wasn't in the least put out by the volume one tiny pair of lungs could generate.

'Oh! Opera singer he is going to be, *ja*?' she laughed the first time she heard it.

'If he ever learns to sing in tune,' agreed Jess wryly.

'But yes. Wagner, I think—very good he would be.'

Sam was working very hard. He had half a dozen contracts scattered around the country, and several more abroad. Sometimes he would be away for several days at a time, and Jess found that she missed him dreadfully. But when he returned home she had to hide all but the tiniest part of her joy on seeing him, and be glad that he was too busy to find the time to look for other diversions beyond her ever-welcoming arms.

He had spoken the truth when he had told her that their first night had been just a beginning. He had taught her pleasures undreamed of, and she no longer resented it when he called her Jezebel. She enjoyed being his mistress, and when they were making love she could forget the circumstances that had made her his wife.

And even when they weren't in bed, things were far better between them than she had dared hope. It was quite impossible to lose her temper with him—he would always make her laugh instead. She had found that she was beginning to share his taste for jazz, and had been with him several times to a dimly lit club round the back of Wardour Street—but so far she had drawn the line at accompanying him to a rugby match.

She would have liked to have had another baby, but she knew that that would have meant risking months when she wasn't at her best, and he might be lured away. So she quietly made her own arrangements, promising herself that if the day ever came when she could start to feel secure, her waistline would be the first thing to go.

Whenever he had some free time, they went house-hunting. But Jess was appalled by the prices. Even a modest three-bedroomed semi on the wrong side of the river was quoted at a king's ransom. 'We're not paying that, Sam,' she protested, aghast. 'Why, the garden's just about big enough to grow one rose-bush in, and if that isn't damp on that back-bedroom wall I've got two heads!'

'Not up to much, is it?' he agreed. 'But it seems about an average price for around here.'

'Average? It's extortion!'

She was tired and dispirited by the time they got back to the hotel. They had been there for nearly seven weeks, and she knew they couldn't stay indefinitely—and it wasn't fair on Sam to have to drag around estate agents in the little time he had to relax.

'I'm sorry we've had a wasted afternoon,' she said. 'But really—that place was horrible.'

'I quite agree with you,' he responded, kicking off his shoes and stretching out on the sofa to read the newspaper.

'You have to be an oil millionaire to be able to afford anything half-way decent in London these days.'

'We could always move out of London,' he suggested tentatively.

Her eyes lit up. 'Live in the country? Oh, I'd love to!'

He looked at her in surprise. 'Would you? I'd have suggested it before, but I thought you wanted to stay in town.'

'Not a bit. It would be lovely for little Sam to grow up in the country. But won't it be inconvenient for you to get to your office—when you've got one?'

'I might not have my office in London. It might be more practical to have it somewhere else.'

She sat forward in eager interest. 'Like where?'

'Oh, I was thinking of somewhere in the Midlands.'

She wrinkled her nose in disgust. 'The Midlands! But you said the country.'

'What about Shropshire?'

'Where's that?'

He laughed at her. 'Don't you know the geography of your own country?' he teased.

'Yes, but . . .it's near Gloucestershire or something, isn't it? That's not the Midlands—nowhere near it.'

'You're miles out!' he chided her. 'It's between Birmingham and mid-Wales. And it's very pretty—I was up there last week.'

'So where would you have your office?' she asked.

'There's a place on the river called Ironbridge—you'd like it, it's all twisty little streets running up the side of the hill. We could have a house there, and I could have my office in Telford—it's only a couple of miles away, and it's a new town, so business rents are low.'

'I've never heard of it.'

'Well, why don't we go up there one day next week and have a look around? If you like it, we can move to a hotel up there while we look for a house. We could even have one built if we can't find what we want.'

The following Tuesday they set off early to drive up the motorway to Shropshire. Jess fretted at leaving little Sam for a whole day, but Helga reassured her comfortably. 'Jess, you must not worry. Very good he will be. No trouble. I promise.'

Jess forced herself to smile. 'Yes—I know I can rely on you, Helga. Well, see you this evening—I'll probably give you a ring at lunchtime.'

Helga laughed, and brought the baby to the window, moving his tiny hand to wave goodbye to them as they drove off.

The big car ate up the miles, and Jess dozed a little, opening her eyes briefly to glance in distaste at the chimneys and gasometers of Birmingham, and then closing them again until the smooth acceleration of the car told her that they had left behind the heavy Midlands traffic.

She looked around her in surprise at the rolling green hills. 'Heavens! How long have I been asleep?'

'Not long. We're almost there.'

'Mmm. I like this. This is *real* countryside.'

'It's even nicer where we're going.'

She wasn't sure if she agreed with him at first. They turned off the motorway and drove down a dual carriageway. 'It's all factories and roundabouts,' she protested.

'We're not there yet,' he told her, laughing.

They drove on around the edge of the town, and down a steep hill, and suddenly they were in the bottom of a wooded gorge, with quaint old houses rising above them, and a sparkling, fast-flowing river to their left. 'Oh, stop! Stop the car! I want to look,' she insisted.

He found a parking space in front of a row of small shops, and Jess scrambled out and ran across the road. An elegant bridge, supported by a delicate framework of semi-circular arches, spanned the river, and Jess ran to the middle of it to look back up at the village.

Georgian houses with their beautifully proportioned windows, sturdy Victorian cottages of brown brick, and a pretty little church with a square tower nestled among the trees that climbed the steep hillside. Below her the river burbled between its grassy banks. The air was still crisp with the chill of winter, but the sky was blue, and every twig and branch knew that spring wasn't far away.

Sam was smiling as he strolled towards her, his hands deep in the pockets of his sheepskin coat. 'I gather you like it,' he remarked.

'Oh, Sam, it's lovely!' she breathed, her eyes sparkling as she looked up at him. 'Can we really live here?'

'Of course, if you want to.' He took a folded sheaf of papers from his pocket. 'I had some of the local estate agents send me details of a few properties. We can go and have a look around now if you like.'

Jess fell in love with the third house they looked at. It was a semi-derelict stone cottage, surrounded by trees, high on the hill overlooking the gorge. Sam pushed open the badly warped front door, and they stepped into a wide hall, with rooms leading off each side.

'Oh, what a pity it's been so neglected,' sighed Jess, wandering through one of the doorways. 'Look at that view! And this room's enormous—it would make a lovely drawing-room. If you could cut down that dead tree, the sunlight would stream in.'

'We could certainly do something with it,' agreed Sam, brushing a cobweb from his jacket. 'The foundations are solid, and there's nothing wrong with the actual walls. It'll need a whole new roof, and I dare say every bit of wood will have to be stripped out and replaced.'

'Could we do it?' pleaded Jess, breathless with excitement.

'Oh, we can do it all right, if you don't mind living in a hotel for another couple of months while the work's done.'

'I don't mind a bit,' agreed Jess, gazing around the room, and planning in her mind just how it would look when it was finished.

'How about some lunch?' Sam suggested. 'I don't know about you, but I'm starving.'

'So am I. It must be all this fresh country air. You know, once all those straggly bushes are cleared away, we could make a nice stretch of lawn out there for little Sam to play on when he gets bigger. I'd like to build him a sand-pit. And here in the front garden we could have roses.'

'Come on,' laughed Sam, taking her arm and drawing her back towards the car. 'You've got all the time in the world to decide what's going where.'

'I must ring Helga.'

'Lunch first. We can have it at the hotel, and see about booking rooms.'

* * *

'Helga? How's he been?'

'As good as gold,' came Helga's placid voice over the phone. 'I told you, you should not worry so. He will be all right without you for just one day.'

Jess laughed at herself for fussing so much—but it was the first time she had been away from him, and if anything should happen to him ... 'We'll be home about six,' she told her. 'It's absolutely fabulous up here, Helga, and we've found the house we're going to buy. It's a tip at the moment, it needs an awful lot doing to it, so I'm afraid it's more hotels for a while.'

'That will not be a problem—Sam and I will not mind. Oh—nearly I forgot—there was a message for your husband. He is to ring the Derbyshire site as soon as possible—very urgent, they said.'

Jess turned and handed Sam the phone. 'There's an urgent message for you,' she said anxiously.

He took the phone. 'Yes ... OK, fine ... no, I know the number. Bye, Helga. Kiss little Sam for me.' He put the phone down. 'Sorry, Jess. They've got a problem on the site,' he said. 'I'll give them a ring. Go back to the table and get us another coffee, would you?'

She nodded, and went back to the table in the dining-room where they had just eaten an excellent lunch. Sam rejoined her a few minutes later, and he was frowning. 'What's the problem?' she asked.

'It's that hypermarket we're building up in Derbyshire. They've got a problem with subsidence. But there shouldn't be subsidence there. Unless ...'

'Unless what?'

'Sometimes there are mines that aren't shown on any records. A few of the landowners in the nineteenth century were pretty devious when it came to avoiding taxation. They honeycombed under their land, sold the coal secretly, and no one was any the wiser. It's only when you try to put a building on top that you find you've got a problem.'

'So it could be serious?'

He nodded. 'I'd better go and take a look. Do you mind? It isn't all that far from here, and it won't make us much later getting home.'

'No...of course,' she agreed readily. Little Sam would be all right with Helga for a few hours longer.

It was a pleasant drive across the country into Derbyshire. The rich hillsides were covered with farmland, and the hedgerows and stone walls still painted a patchwork picture of the heart of England which had remained unchanged for centuries.

Sam drew the car to a halt outside the site office. The hypermarket building was almost finished, a three-storey monstrosity of concrete that marred the green landscape in which it stood.

'Who on earth designed that?' Jess enquired, wrinkling her nose in distaste.

'Ugly, isn't it?' agreed Sam. 'It's the modern school, I believe.'

'There's modern and modern,' declared Jess with a touch of asperity. 'That looks as if it was designed by a fifth-former trying to re-invent the match-box. I hope it does fall down.'

Sam laughed. 'I won't be long,' he promised. 'I'll just see if I can get some idea of what we're up against.'

Jess got out of the car, and leaned against it, gazing out at the scenery. On the other side of a low stone wall a brown and white cow was placidly chewing on a tuft of long grass, her liquid brown eyes seeming to cry for the destruction of her lovely valley by the advent of that grotesque lump of architecture.

She turned, and a very different scene met her eyes. Bulldozers and concrete mixers had torn up the grass and turned it to a sea of grey-brown mud. The grey metal prefabricated huts used by the workmen looked like some ugly barracks, and there were piles of sand and girders like pock-marks all over the place. And above it, like some evil queen, presided the pallid concrete mass of the hypermarket.

Sam had put on a hard-hat, and was walking along the side of the building with the site-manager, examining the wall closely. Jess could see the problem. A pattern of cracks had formed at the stress points, suggesting that the foundations were sinking in one corner. They would have to dig right down beneath...

There was a strange, deep rumbling noise, and as Jess watched in a kind of frozen fascination the whole wall began to tip outwards, and then came cascading down in an earthquake of rubble—engulfing the two men standing below.

'Sam!' She was running while everyone else seemed to be rooted to the spot, her own scream echoing in her ears. The rubble was still slipping as she scrambled over it, heaving aside great lumps of concrete that she could never have lifted without the superhuman strength of panic. She didn't feel the pain as she tore her hands on the sharp edges, digging frantically at the spot where she knew he lay.

She found his arm, and then his head, tears streaming down her dust-grimed face as she scrabbled to make the hole bigger. 'Sam!' she sobbed, reaching out to touch his face.

He lifted his head, coughing a little, blinking at the daylight. Then his eyes focused on her face and he smiled a little crookedly. 'You look a mess,' he murmured.

Relief engulfed her, so that she didn't know whether to laugh or cry. 'Oh, Sam, you big ape,' she breathed. 'I thought you'd been killed. If I lost you again...'

He reached up his hand and touched away one tear-drop. 'It's wet,' he teased gently. 'That's a brilliant trick. How did you do it? If I didn't know you better I could almost believe that it was a real tear.'

'Sam, don't,' she sobbed, catching his hand and pressing it to her lips. 'I love you.'

He stroked her cheek with the backs of his fingers. 'When did you finally work that out?' he enquired.

'I've loved you all along,' she confessed in a shaking voice. 'Right from the beginning, before we were even married.'

He chuckled softly. 'And I thought I was the only one that was crazy.'

Suddenly he groaned, and his face twisted in pain. 'Sam...!' She glanced around desperately for help. The first of the workmen had finally caught up with her. 'He's hurt. Get a doctor,' she begged urgently.

'They're ringing for an ambulance now,' he assured her. 'It'll be here in no time.' He leaned forward cautiously. 'Sam? What's the damage, old son?'

Sam opened his eyes again. 'I think my leg's broken, and maybe my shoulder and a couple of ribs as well.'

'Well, hang on in there. The doc'll be here soon.'

'How's Terry?'

'They're just pulling him out now. Nothing but a couple of bruises.'

Sam smiled wryly. 'Luck of the Irish.'

A car swept round on to the site, and pulled up with a crunch at the base of the pile of rubble. 'Ah, here's Dr Patel,' announced the workman with relief. 'That was quick—he must have got a call on the radio.'

The doctor was a young man, but he had an air of brisk competence that was reassuring. He climbed nimbly over the rubble, and knelt down beside Jess. 'Right,' he said to Sam. 'Let me have a look at you.'

'He said he's broken his leg, his shoulder and a couple of ribs,' the workman told him.

The doctor nodded. 'Uh-huh. Has he coughed up any blood?'

'No,' put in Jess.

'Good. How many fingers am I holding up?' he asked Sam.

'Three.'

'Very good. Now, I'm just going to shine a light into your eyes for a second, OK?' His examination was swift but thorough, and then he sat back on his heels. 'Good. Well, it seems as though he's been quite lucky,' he said to Jess. 'I'm going to give him an injection for the pain. Once we have him out on to a stretcher I shall be able to examine him properly.'

As he was talking he was preparing a hypodermic syringe, and with no waste of time he slid it into the back of Sam's hand. 'There. It's quite a strong injection—I'm hoping it will make him go to sleep. It isn't going to be very nice for him to be moved out of this hole.'

Jess could feel Sam begin to relax at once, and the lines of pain eased out of his face. As the doctor moved away he opened his eyes again, and looked up at her. 'Jess?'

'I'm here,' she reassured him quickly.

'I'm sorry, Jess,' he murmured, 'I messed everything up between us, didn't I?'

'It was my fault as much as yours.' She squeezed his hand. 'But it doesn't matter now. We'll have plenty of time to make it up to each other.'

'Yes.' He sighed. 'I judged you all wrong, right from the beginning,' he went on, his voice so quiet that she had to lean down close to him to catch what he was saying. 'I thought you were just a red-head with no heart, and I was a fool to fall in love with you.''

Tears were stinging the backs of her eyes again. 'Oh, Sam,' she whispered softly. 'I wish I'd known that. Why didn't you tell me?'

'And have you walk all over me? Not likely—not until I'd heard you say it first.'

She smiled wistfully. 'I was going to tell you—that first Christmas. But you spent it with Lisa instead.'

He stared at her, puzzled. 'I didn't. I spent it with friends. I got back to the office party after giving some of the kids from the typing-pool a lift home, and you'd gone, and you weren't at the flat, either. I waited for hours—in the end I got a bit mad, and went off to another party on my own. I bumped into some people I used to know—they didn't know I was married. They invited me to spend Christmas with them, so I did—I thought you'd be doing your own thing.'

'Oh!' She knew he was telling the truth. 'But you were having an affair with Lisa, weren't you?' she persisted sadly.

He managed a mischievous grin. 'I almost did for a while,' he admitted. 'But only to make you jealous. I thought it had worked, too, when you asked me to marry you. But instead things were worse than ever.'

'So you went back to Lisa.'

'No I didn't—not after we were married.'

'What about New Year's Eve?' she challenged.

'Oh...that.' The sedative was beginning to take effect. 'You were with that damned cousin of hers all evening. I wanted to knock his damned teeth down his throat. But Lisa wouldn't let me spoil her party. She dragged me off downstairs.' He smiled weakly. 'You should have come and rescued me,' he murmured. 'She was practically raping me.'

'It didn't look to me as if you were exactly fighting to get away,' she told him with a touch of asperity. He looked up at her enquiringly. 'I came looking for you. When I saw you with her...'

He shook his head. 'Nothing happened, Jess,' he promised. 'She wasn't you. It was only you I wanted. It didn't go any further.'

'Then why did you leave me?'

'I had to. I was going out of my head. After what happened...I never meant it to be like that...I just seemed to snap. I knew I had to get away from you— as far away as I could.' His voice was growing fainter. 'I thought a year in the jungle must have cured me, so I came back. I was going to give you your divorce...but then, when I found out you'd had a baby...'

'Was it just for him you wanted me back, Sam?' she pleaded.

He looked up into her eyes. 'You know it wasn't,' he murmured. 'I've been aching to hear you say what you said just now. Say it again, Jess.'

She smiled down at him happily. 'I love you, Sam,' she breathed.

He sighed with contentment, and closed his eyes. His breathing had taken on a deeper rhythm, and she realized that he was hovering on the fringes of consciousness. Behind her the ambulance and fire brigade had arrived, and in seconds they were all around her, considering the best way to excavate the hole and get him out.

One of them leaned over her. 'You ought to go and wait down by the ambulance, where it's safe,' he advised her gently.

She looked up quickly. 'Oh, please,' she begged, 'if I won't be in the way, I'd rather stay with him.'

'Oh, you won't be in the way, but ...'

'Then let me stay.'

Sam opened his eyes briefly. 'Let her stay,' he murmured. His eyes closed again, and with the last of his strength as the anaesthetic took effect he drew her hand down to his lips. 'Always...'

EPILOGUE

JESS reached up to put the finishing touches to the Christmas tree. It looked lovely, here in the traditional setting of their newly restored cottage high above the Ironbridge Gorge. It reached almost to the ceiling, and the green branches were heavily laden with tinsel. Underneath were all the presents, brightly wrapped in Christmas paper.

The silver fairy on top looked as if she had already been imbibing the Christmas spirit, so Jess clambered on to a chair to straighten her.

'Do you really think you ought to be doing that in your condition?'

She turned quickly. 'Sam! Oh, I was so keeping my fingers crossed you'd be home in time for Christmas! How did it go? Did you get the contract?'

'It was a cinch,' he told her, dropping his coat and briefcase and strolling across the room to lift her down from the chair and greet her with a warm, lingering kiss. 'Have you missed me?'

Her eyes danced as she smiled up at him. 'Oh, well...maybe a bit, now and then,' she teased.

'You'd better thank heaven for your lump,' he advised her, 'otherwise I'd put you over my knee.' His eyes were warm with pride as he held her at arm's length to survey her no-longer slender figure.

She gurgled with laughter, hugging his arm and drawing him down beside her on the comfortable sofa.

'So what have you been doing with yourself while I've been away?' he wanted to know.

'Well, I've finished painting the new baby's nursery, and I've iced the Christmas cake, and I've made *dozens* of mince pies...'

'You haven't been overdoing it, have you?'

'Of course not. Do you realise, this is the third Christmas we've been married, and it's the first time we've spent it together? So long as the results of your rapid recovery from all those broken bones nine months ago doesn't ruin it for us,' she added wryly, patting her round tummy.

'I don't think it'll ruin it at all,' he declared, nestling her comfortably into the crook of his arm. 'I think it would be a lovely way to spend Christmas.'

'It's all right for you,' she protested. 'All you've got to do is hold my hand and mop my brow.'

'I shall probably faint.'

She struck his wide chest with her fist. 'Don't you dare!' she warned fiercely.

He grinned, hugging her close. 'I won't,' he promised. 'I'm not going to miss one second of this. I missed everything with little Sam. If the flight from Munich had been delayed, I think I'd have swum across the Channel.'

She smiled contentedly, resting her head on his shoulder. 'It wouldn't have been delayed,' she told him confidently. 'I'd fixed it with my magic spell—I'm the Christmas fairy.'

'You're the pregnantest Christmas fairy I've ever seen.'

She cast him a look of laughing indignation. '"Pregnantest"?' she repeated. 'What sort of word is that?'

'It means superlatively pregnant, which is what you are.' He kissed her nose. 'You're absolutely beautiful.'

'I'm absolutely enormous,' she said with a sigh.

'Mmm,' he agreed, surveying her lump speculatively. 'Are you *sure* it isn't twins?'

She rolled her eyes. 'Heavens, the last little demon you sired was quite enough—I'm not sure I could cope with two at once.'

'Helga would be delighted.'

'Helga is an accredited saint, and I'm more than thankful that she's agreed to stay on with us. I don't know what... Ow!'

He looked down at her anxiously. 'What is it?'

'I got a twinge in my back,' she grumbled, trying to sit up.

'The baby?'

'No...it was just the way I was sitting.' But she had her doubts. She had been restless all day, unable to sit still, fiddling with things in the kitchen until Helga had told her off.

She had another twinge of pain, half an hour after the first, and twenty-five minutes later felt another one, stronger this time. The next time, Sam caught her glancing at the clock. 'How long?' he demanded.

'Twenty minutes.'

He went white. 'What? We'd better get going! Where's your bag? Where did I put the car keys—or would you rather I rang for an ambulance?'

She laughed complacently at his agitation. 'Don't panic,' she soothed. 'The bag's beside the front door, and your keys are where you left them—on top of your briefcase. I'm going to see if little Sam's woken up from his nap yet, so that I can kiss him goodbye.'

'Oh, for heaven's sake—there isn't time! Why didn't you tell me before?'

She stood on tiptoe to wrap her arms around his neck, and plant an affectionate kiss on the end of his nose. 'Will you stop flapping?' she chided gently. 'It'll be ages yet—it probably won't arrive until tomorrow—Christmas Day!'

He smiled down at her lovingly. 'I'm sorry. But you're one very important lady to me, and I don't want anything to go wrong.'

'Nothing's going to go wrong. I told you—I'm the Christmas fairy.'

The hospital was bright with Christmas decorations, and somewhere they could hear carol-singers. The staff on the maternity unit welcomed them cheerfully. '*Another* one! Everyone's decided to have Christmas presents this year.'

The midwife, whom Jess had already met, came round from the nurses' station, her broad face smiling. 'Come along then, Mrs Ryder. Let's get you settled in, and then we can see how things are getting on. How close are your pains?'

'Every ten minutes now.'

'Good—it shouldn't be too long then. Here we are—pop out of your things, and pop up on the bed. Just ring the bell when you're ready, and I'll be along.'

She drew the curtains round the bed, and left them alone. Jess glanced up at Sam, suddenly rather nervous. 'Well, this is it,' she murmured.

His eyes were shadowed with anxiety. 'How are you feeling?' he asked.

'On edge. I suppose I'd better put this thing on,' she added, picking up the hospital robe. 'Heavens, it's like a marquee! Which way do I get into it?'

She had to pause while another pain gripped her. 'That wasn't ten minutes,' said Sam.

'No—more like five,' she agreed, her eyes wide. 'Quick, help me into this thing, and buzz for the midwife.'

But the smiling young woman was already back. 'How are we doing?' she enquired briskly.

'Five minutes this time,' Jess told her.

'Really? Well, perhaps we'd better get you straight into the delivery room. Is your husband staying?'

'Yes,' put in Sam firmly.

'Well, you'll have to put a robe on then. Come on, Mrs Ryder. Do you want to walk, or shall I fetch a chair?'

'I'll walk,' said Jess, gripping her arm for support. 'Ow! Make that run!'

'This isn't your first, is it?' the midwife asked in a friendly tone as she led her across the corridor.

'No, my second.'

'How long was your labour last time?'

'About eight hours, I think. This one's going to be much quicker.'

'It often is, the second time. Here you are—up we go.'

Jess lay back on the delivery table, and looked around for Sam. He appeared a moment later, swathed in a green hospital robe, a disposable paper cap on his head. Jess laughed up at him teasingly, but then another pain came, and she gladly accepted the offer of gas and air.

After that everything dissolved into a blur. The only reality in the world seemed to be Sam's grey eyes, and his soft voice, coaxing her through the pain. She did just as she was told, and suddenly there was a loud cry that made her heart leap. She struggled to sit up and look. 'Is it all right?'

'She's perfect,' Sam whispered, squeezing her shoulder as the midwife laid the tiny, wet red-faced bundle on her chest.

'Ohh!' She put up her hand to stroke the damp hair, as Sam stroked the round cheek with his finger. 'She's...ow!'

'What...?'

'I don't think we've finished,' the midwife said, amazed laughter in her voice. Sam stared at her, and she smiled at him apologetically. 'I'm sorry. Even in these days of advanced medical science, they still manage to fool us sometimes!'

'You mean it *is* twins?' gasped Jess.

The midwife nodded, smiling.

'Twins?' An expression of pure delight crossed Sam's face. 'Are you sure?'

'Definitely.'

'Are you ever going to stop admiring your daughters?'

Sam smiled back at Jess as she lay back on the pillows, exhausted but extremely proud of herself.

'No, why should I? They're the most beautiful babies in the world.'

Jess chuckled. 'All babies are beautiful to their fathers.'

'But these two really are—they take after their mother.' He leaned down over the bed and kissed her. 'Do you know something, Mrs Ryder? I'm glad you asked me to marry you.'

Jess wrapped her arms around his neck, pulling him down for another kiss.

'And do you know something, Mr Ryder? I'm glad you accepted.'

If *YOU* enjoyed this book,
your daughter may enjoy

Romances from

CROSSWINDS

Keepsake is a series of tender, funny, down-to-earth romances for younger teens.

The simple boy-meets-girl romances have lively and believable characters, lots of action and romantic situations with which teens can identify.

Available now wherever books are sold.

Harlequin American Romance

Romances that go one step farther...
American Romance

Realistic stories involving people you can relate to and care about.

Compelling relationships between the mature men and women of today's world.

Romances that capture the core of genuine emotions between a man and a woman.

Join us each month for four new titles wherever paperback books are sold.
Enter the world of American Romance.

Amro-1